RED PINES

JILL HAND

Black Rose Writing | Texas

ISBN: 978-1-68513-401-3
LIBRARY OF CONGRESS CONTROL NUMBER: 2023949153
PUBLISHED BY BLACK ROSE WRITING
www.blackrosewriting.com

Printed in the United States of America
Suggested Retail Price (SRP) $17.95

Red Pines is printed in Calluna

Dives aut iniquus est aut iniqui hæres
Desiderius Erasmus, Praise of Folly

Red Pines

PROLOGUE
NIGHT GARDEN

Janet Marietta Castleberry stamped her boot on the spade's metal tread. With a grunt of effort, she lifted a load of red dirt and heaved it onto the growing pile beside the deep trench in which she stood.

Janet was planting by the dark of the moon. Over the years, she had gleaned a considerable amount of horticultural information from *The Old Farmer's Almanac*. That venerable publication claims the dark of the moon is the best time to plant flowering bulbs such as tulips and daffodils, as well as potatoes and other vegetables that bear crops below ground. Plant when the moon is on the wane, the *Almanac* advises, and whatever you're planting won't all go to top.

What Janet was planting that warm spring night in Georgia was in no danger of sprouting green shoots, the way onions do. It could, however, attract wild animals. The field where she was working was a stone's throw from the Chattahoochee National Forest, the largest national forest east of the Mississippi. Bears and coyotes prowl its mountains and woodlands, as well as foxes and feral swine. That's why Janet was digging such a deep hole.

Stomp. Lift. Throw. Stomp. Lift. Throw. Strands of gray hair clung damply to her forehead. She was miserably aware that her cotton shirt, fresh as a daisy when she put it on that morning, was now sweat-soaked and streaked with dirt. Breathing the humid air was like trying to inhale a hot, muddy mist through a wool blanket.

"Whew," she panted. "I'm glad I don't have to do this for a living."

One hole was dug and planted. The second, final one, was almost done. It had taken her hours. The first pale glimmer of dawn was beginning to brighten the horizon. With her work almost complete, she looked forward to finishing up and going home. She'd scrape the mud off her boots and make a cup of tea. Then she'd ease her aching body into a hot bath.

A mosquito buzzed past her ear, landing on her arm. She slapped it, smashing it flat. She had rolled her shirtsleeves to the elbows to allow for more freedom of movement before she began digging, and the mosquitos and no-see-ums swarmed around her in a buzzing black cloud. There was a spray bottle of insect repellant in her truck, but Janet was determined not to go and get it. Once in the truck, she'd be tempted to drive home. She mustn't do that, not yet. Not until her task was complete.

Aside from the crunching of Janet's spade, the only sound was that of the wind soughing through the branches of the trees in the nearby forest, and the angry screech of an owl as it attempted to drive a red-tailed hawk from its territory. The nearest house was half a mile away, its windows dark, the occupants having long since retired for the night.

Janet and her late husband, Roger Castleberry, had purchased the field from a man who had planted it with red pines. The trees, with their crinkly, pale red bark and straight trunks, were in demand for use as utility poles. Janet and Roger sold the pines to a logging company and had blueprints drawn up for a cabin. They looked forward to spending their golden years there, fishing and birdwatching and just taking it easy, relaxing on the front porch in rocking chairs. Then Roger dropped dead of a heart attack at his retirement party and there went that plan.

There were some who blamed Roger's sudden death on the cake provided by Suzanne's Blessed Christian Bakery. There was nothing particularly devout about either Suzanne or her bakery. The name was chosen in a calculated attempt to lure customers who would believe they were doing the Lord's work by buying baked goods there.

GOODBYE, YOU OLD FART! was written in black icing on Roger's fatal retirement cake. As a finishing touch, a life-size skeletal hand, sculpted from fondant, raised its middle finger in an insolent salute.

Roger stared in shock as the cake was wheeled out on a cart into the dining room reserved for his sendoff at the Happy Traveler Inn & Suites (free Wi-Fi, HBO and shuttle service to the airport.) The guests just about split their sides, laughing at his stunned expression. The laughter abruptly ceased when Roger collapsed to the floor, stone dead, still clutching the cake knife.

It turned out he had a bad ticker, a condition the existence of which neither Roger nor his doctor was aware. The cake wasn't to blame for his dramatic demise, although its flippant message and charnel house decoration, intended in good fun by his playful coworkers, were criticized for being tasteless.

The log cabin never became a reality. Janet's friends tried to talk her into selling the land, but she stubbornly refused. She had a sentimental attachment to it. It was where she'd buried the urn containing Roger's ashes. She'd made a memorial garden, planting it with magenta Charles de Mills roses. It was an old rose, its history reaching all the way back to ancient Greek and Roman gardens. Janet had carried them in her bridal bouquet when she married Roger. She could smell their lush fragrance now, as she dug.

Janet was strong; a lifetime of exercising and eating right had kept her in shape. Still, she was seventy-three, prone to the aches and pains inherent in just about everyone who's put that much mileage on the odometer. The muscles in her lower back complained, letting her know she'd barely be able to walk tomorrow.

Judging the hole to be deep enough and long enough to hold the object waiting beside it, Janet tossed the spade out, then hoisted herself up and out.

"That's that," she said, brushing dirt from her gloved hands. She bent over the man's lifeless body, being careful not to wrench her back, and rolled the corpse into the hole. It landed with a thump, facedown in the dirt. Janet studied it for a moment before taking up her spade. As she filled in the grave, she sang a song from her girlhood.

"Where have all the flowers gone?" she sang, as she shoveled red dirt over the second and final corpse.

CHAPTER ONE - HUBRIS

Aimee Trapnell drew admiring stares as she sauntered along West Seventy-second Street. She was fresh from the hair salon, her chin-length, chestnut-colored hair having been treated with chemicals until it assumed a blinding shine not ordinarily seen outside of shampoo commercials. Tall, razor-thin and brimming with self-confidence, Aimee was smugly aware of her splendid visual impact.

Unlike her brother, Marsh, who was a scholar, among other things, Aimee was unfamiliar with Greek tragedy. She had never heard of the concept of hubris, in which the character flaws of extreme pride, ambition and haughtiness so offend the gods that it leads to one's downfall. Aimee was soon to get a harsh lesson in hubris, but at that moment, she was blissfully unaware that her life was about to take a turn for the worse.

She was dressed head to toe in garments made by Clobber. It was her own brand, with most of the clothing and accessories designed by Aimee personally. Clobber was known for not only flouting the conventions of good taste, but for defiantly trampling on them. Today, her form-fitting white t-shirt featured a disgusting image of a hummingbird being swallowed, tail-end first, by a bullfrog. The little bird's beak was wide open and its tongue outthrust. Its eyes bulged, as if begging for mercy, which would not be forthcoming.

Written underneath was EMBRACE THE JOY OF THE MOMENT.

Aimee's tiny linen skirt was frayed at the hem and had several strategic rips fore and aft. The skirt and top looked as though they might have come from a charity bin, but appearances were deceiving. Clothing made by Clobber sold for astronomical sums in boutiques in Manhattan, London, Paris, Shanghai, Dubai, Seoul, Hong Kong, and Zurich. Forget Prada. Forget Chanel. Forget Armani. Clobber was currently the hottest designer brand.

Aimee had emerged from the subway station swinging an emerald-green shopping bag filled with lotions and unguents from Kirei's flagship store on Third Avenue. She could have had her driver pick her up, but every so often she liked to take the subway. Sometimes buskers would be performing on the platform, juggling fruit, or singing arias or playing a musical instrument. Aimee, who had only a vague idea of what it was like not to have unlimited funds at one's disposal, found it odd that they would go to so much trouble for some spare change.

Unlike her friends, who wouldn't be caught dead riding the subway, she liked to do it on occasion, just for variety, but only for one or two stops in the better neighborhoods.

This time, Aimee's visit to Manhattan's subterranean transportation system had been prompted by the fact that the cars on the IND Eighth Avenue line had placards inside them, advertising her latest endeavor, a perfume called Night Garden.

In addition to the subway placards and ads in print magazines and online, there was a television commercial for Night Garden, teasingly shown only once. In it, a bedraggled young woman climbed into a dumpster in an alley. It was night, the scene stippled with shadows, a full moon riding high and lonely above tenement rooftops. The woman dug through bags of trash until she found a grilled chicken wing with some meat left on it. She devoured it hungrily, staring into the camera, her bleak expression the epitome of hopelessness. A siren wailed, *whoop-whooping,* coming closer before receding into the distance, its pitch changing with a Doppler effect.

That part of the commercial was in grainy black and white, poorly framed, as if filmed by a novice with a hand-held camera. It made one wonder what was going on. Was it some kind of public-service announcement? Perhaps a plea for donations to fight drug addiction or homelessness?

Having finished with the chicken, the woman tossed the bone away. Once again, she rooted through the trash. This time she came up with a round crystal bottle: a perfume atomizer. She gazed wonderingly at it, a streetlight illuminating it in such a way as to make it sparkle like something rare and precious. Then she held it to her wrist and pumped the rubber bulb.

Instantly, the scene changed, becoming flooded with radiant color. The effect was magical in movie theaters in 1939, when audiences watching *The Wizard of Oz* saw Dorothy and her companions enter the Emerald City. It was just as magical now, as the pathetic homeless woman became a diva in a fabulous gown, emerging from a stretch limousine onto a red carpet lined with paparazzi and a cheering, jostling crowd of people holding up smart phones.

A voiceover solemnly intoned, "Night Garden. It will transform you."

The commercial was fifteen seconds long and cost ten million dollars. Much of that went to the actor whose deep, gravelly voice, recognizable practically anywhere in the world, spoke those six words. Shown only once, the expense seemed profligate, but like everything Aimee did, it was for a reason, in this case, to create a buzz.

It worked even better than she had hoped. Not since Apple's "1984" commercial for the original Mcintosh computer had a television ad been the topic of so much excited conversation.

The Night Garden commercial was praised for drawing attention to homeless women and empowering them. Conversely, it was criticized for drawing attention to homeless women and trivializing them. As a result, everyone wanted to try Night Garden, to find out whether it would transform *them*.

Night Garden lacked the ability to produce miraculous transformations. However, it did something almost as good; it imparted a sense of superiority upon its wearers. They felt they were better than they'd been before, simply by owning a bottle.

What did Night Garden smell like? It was ambrosial, a combination of night-blooming jasmine, fresh-cut hay, and oud, with a powdery vanilla undertone. It was created by a master perfumer, the great-grandson of the founder of a venerable Paris fragrance house which occupied the ground floor of a building on the Rue du Mont Thabor.

The perfume house was the source of Aimee's private scent, made expressly for her and available only to her. Its scent was reminiscent of rich, black earth in which lilies grew, as well as creosote and ozone and hot metal. It was portentous and a little frightening, like the electrically charged air just before a thunderstorm. If a perfume can be said to be an interpretation of one's personality, then it was exactly right for Aimee.

A one-ounce bottle of Night Garden retailed for two hundred and fifty dollars. Despite its hefty price, it was selling like hotcakes. Its launch was so successful that plans were underway for a line of Aimee Trapnell-brand cosmetics. If those were well received, there would be luxury bedding and home furnishings, followed, perhaps, by cookware. Not that Aimee ever cooked. She had people who did that for her.

The world was Aimee's oyster as she approached the Dakota, where she owned two residences. The building's distinctive, angular gothic gables pointed skyward at the corner of Seventy-second Street and Central Park West, making it one of the city's most recognizable landmarks, as well as one of its most prestigious addresses. Aimee advanced upon it, shoulders back, head held high, swinging her shopping bag, her high heels tapping a brisk, staccato rhythm on the sidewalk. Heads turned to watch her regal progress.

Aimee had much to be pleased about that spring morning. In addition to the success of Clobber and Night Garden, two highly eligible bachelors had forsworn spending that summer in the Hamptons in order to dance attendance on her. They escorted her to openings at art galleries and to lunches at the River Club. They took her to little bistros in the Village done up like English pubs or Italian trattorias. They took her to hear the New York Philharmonic String Quartette perform at The Cloisters, and to black-tie events for patrons of the Metropolitan Museum of Art. They flattered her. They bought her gifts. They hung on her every word, as if mesmerized. In short, they did everything in their power to ingratiate themselves.

There were intimate dinners at sidewalk cafés, a bottle of Champagne chilling tableside in a stainless-steel ice bucket beaded with condensation. Her middle-aged swains would hold her hand and murmur endearments as car horns blatted and a hot wind gusted down the Manhattan canyons.

Divorced once, widowed once, Aimee was in no hurry to commit fully to another romantic entanglement. She basked in the attention of her two gentlemen callers, deftly avoiding their pleas to take the relationship to the next level. It would mean becoming formally engaged. It would mean an announcement in the *New York Times*. It would mean one of the two gentlemen would have to be shown the door. She didn't want to do that. She liked leaving her options open.

Her life, at that moment, was all she could wish for. She took a deep breath, savoring the typical Upper West Side scent of exhaust fumes and hot asphalt and the occasional whiff of cigar smoke and expensive aftershave. Aimee would have recognized this heady olfactory brew anywhere, even if she were blindfolded. It was the scent of moneyed Manhattan.

She passed through pockets of cold air, as the doors of shops selling luxury goods opened to allow customers access or egress. Some of those customers, Aimee was pleased to note, wore Clobber.

From beneath her feet came the muffled rumble of the subway. In the street, taxicabs and delivery trucks inched forward. It was the same old, same old, another day, another traffic jam. Irritable drivers of passenger cars, regretting not having taken public transportation, honked their horns in frustration. Cursing, they searched in vain for a place to park. Across the street, in Central Park, trees spread their leafy green canopies, creating a cool, inviting haven on this unseasonably warm spring day.

This is going to be the best summer of my life. I can feel it, Aimee thought.

That's when she noticed the broadcast vehicles parked at the curb in front of the Dakota, double-parked, some of them. Reporters and cameramen milled around, talking into their phones. Heavy black electrical cables snaked along the sidewalk, getting in the way of pedestrians. Something was going on.

Boom operators had their fuzzy microphones on long poles pointed at Hervé, the oldest and most dignified of the Dakota's doormen. Hervé was frowning and holding up his white-gloved hands as if to say, "No comment!"

Aimee sighed, annoyed. She was used to the media besieging the Dakota, due to some scandal or tragedy involving one of the residents. No way was Hervé letting them in. Aimee wondered who was in trouble this time. She thought it might be a certain investment banker, the black sheep member of a dignified old Knickerbocker family from whose loins had sprung three New York State governors and innumerable Wall Street tycoons.

The investment banker was notorious for his drug-fueled escapades, which included punching cab drivers, being thrown out of nightclubs, and running through the streets at 3 a.m., stark naked and screeching like a toucan.

Or it could be the woman known as Baby Patty Cake, BPC to her raucous fans. She was a rapper, originally from Ozone Park, the daughter of postal workers. Baby Patty Cake was famous for getting into feuds with other young female celebrities, starting with Twitter clap-backs and progressing to out-and-out brawls involving bodyguards and entourage members.

Brash, pink-haired, chewing a wad of bubblegum, Baby Patty Cake had entered an elevator at the Dakota one time when Aimee was in there, preparing to ascend to her apartment. The two of them were alone. The building's former elevator operators—women in black dresses with white lace trim—had long since been eliminated from the staff roster. Baby Patty Cake looked Aimee up and down while the little white dog she carried in her purse yapped frantically.

"I know who you are; you're that fashion designer," the rapper said, smacking her gum.

"That's right," Aimee replied, pressing the button for her floor.

"You wanna gimme some clothes?"

"No."

The little dog bared its teeth and growled. "Aw, come on. Don't be stingy. You make clothes. You must have extras. Come on, we're neighbors. You got a crib here, same as me," Baby Patty Cake wheedled.

The overpowering fruity smell of her unwanted companion's bubble gum was making Aimee queasy. "You'll have to contact my publicist. It's not as if I have a closet filled with clothes that I can give away."

That was true. Aimee didn't have a closet filled with clothes that she could give away. She had an entire room. It was chock-full of Clobber merchandise neatly arranged on racks and shelves. There was everything from sunglasses to lingerie to sleepwear to casual wear to sequined dresses suitable for a night of clubbing, all brand-new, with the tags still on. She could, if she wanted to, give some of it to the importuning rapper, but she didn't want to. She didn't like Baby Patty Cake; therefore, Baby Patty Cake would be getting zilch from her.

Baby Patty Cake's eyes narrowed. She glared at Aimee through her eyelash extensions, sending out powerful waves of enmity. She snapped her gum, making a sound like a pistol shot. Chewing furiously, she coaxed the wad into the proper shape and blew a bubble. It grew to the size of a cantaloupe before popping. She stuck the sticky mess back in her mouth, using a finger tipped with a long nail adorned with glittery silver polish.

"Be that way, bitch," she snarled. "Fact is, your clothes are ugly. I was trying to give you a come-up by wearing some of your shit!"

The elevator arrived at Baby Patty Cake's floor. She got out, smiled icily at Aimee, and delivered a final salvo. "You better watch your step, *chica*. One word from me and my homegirls will do the Hucklebuck on your skinny ass."

That was Aimee's sole encounter with Baby Patty Cake. It was enough to make her loathe the pink-haired rapper. Her hopes rose at the sight of the media horde milling around outside the Dakota. Maybe Baby Patty Cake had been arrested or was involved in a revolting scandal, one which would leave her stigmatized forever, a pariah, her music no longer popular, her presence no longer welcomed at award ceremonies.

Aimee edged past the outer fringe of jostling, shouting media people clustered around the twenty-foot-high archway where John Lennon was shot. She'd go upstairs, take a nap, and be rested for her dinner that evening with Leighton Knauss, heir to a frozen foods fortune and one of her two current beaus.

That's when a cameraman shouted, "There she is!"

Aimee looked around in confusion as the media mob converged on her. A woman with an avid, hawklike face and eyebrows like Frida Kahlo's was the first to reach her. Thrusting a microphone at her, the woman said, "Ms. Trapnell! I'm Leticia Guerrero from News 3 New York. What do you have to say about your aunt's arrest in connection with a double murder?"

CHAPTER TWO
UNCLE COURTLAND'S MISTAKE

The twin doors to Aimee's apartment opened onto a spacious vestibule. In turn, the vestibule opened onto a gallery nine feet wide and fourteen feet long. This space, originally intended as a place for visitors to wait before being conducted farther inside, contained twice as much square footage as that of some micro-apartments in Kips Bay or St. Mark's Place.

The gallery was crammed full of flowers, to the point that only a narrow aisle in the center remained to permit passage to the vast living room beyond. The flowers were divided left and right, like guests at a wedding. The ones on the left were from Leighton Knauss, heir to the Friendly Farmer brand frozen food fortune. Forty-five years old, intensely cautious, with a pinched little face like that of a Galapágos tortoise, Knauss considered himself a poet at heart. When ordering flowers to be sent to Aimee, he insisted on them having naturally green blooms. This, he told her, so often that she was heartily sick of hearing it, was a tribute to her startling pale green eyes.

Aimee, pretending to be overcome, would purr, "That's so sweet of you, Leighton. How'd you ever think of something so romantic?" He'd grin foolishly, proud of himself, like a dog that has fetched a stick and is rewarded with a belly rub.

Leighton's viridescent floral love tokens included Limelight hydrangeas, chartreuse gladiolus, *rosa chinensis viridiflora*—a true green rose, not the kind with artificially dyed blossoms that are found wrapped in cellophane at gas stations and bodegas—and green ball dianthus, its fuzzy, lime-green spheres resembling strange flora from another planet.

Mediterranean splurge, hellebore, calla lilies, ranunculus, all green, all were fashioned into extravagant, towering arrangements by the city's best florists. A new one was delivered to Aimee's apartment each day. They had little cards attached on which Leighton poured out his devotion.

"Friendly Farmer foods are frozen, but my heart is on fire with flames of love," said one.

"Roses are red, these flowers are green. You're the prettiest girl that I've ever seen," said another.

The lush scent of fresh flowers, like that of a florist shop or a funeral, struck Aimee as soon as she opened the front door. She strode angrily through the gallery, not even glancing at the bank of green flowers on her left. She likewise ignored the floral tributes clustered on her right. These were from her other admirer, Avery Panko. He was a real-estate developer who had survived the crash of 2008 due to questionable dealings with a certain German bank. So far, those dealings had avoided scrutiny by the Internal Revenue Service.

Avery didn't go in for variety in his choice of flowers, the way his rival, Leighton, did. He invariably sent Aimee long-stemmed red roses, twenty-four to a crystal vase, a new one arriving every day, like clockwork.

Thickly mustached, his dark hair attractively threaded with gray, given to long, smoldering gazes, Avery had a vulpine quality reminiscent of a Lothario from the days of silent films, Rudolph Valentino, perhaps. He'd decided long ago that long-stemmed red roses were the only suitable flowers to give a woman in whom he was interested.

The effect of this tunnel of red and green was that of a shopping mall decorated for Christmas. One expected to see a sign pointing THIS WAY TO SANTA, with a throne on a platform at the end where the Jolly Old Elf would be ensconced.

Aimee's entrance into the living room caused a light to blink in a panel on the wall of the kitchen, where her housekeeper, Mildred Pickering, was taking a batch of scones out of the oven. There were similar lights in the apartment's other twelve rooms, put there for the benefit of Mildred, who was born Deaf. That's how she and other members of the Deaf community referred to it, in uppercase, with its unique language, customs, and experiences forming a bond between them. Mildred could read lips and Aimee had learned American Sign Language in order to communicate with her more easily.

Mildred entered the living room where Aimee stood, one high-heeled shoe irritably tapping on the polished parquet floor. In body language, it was the equivalent of an angry cat twitching its tail. Aimee's back was to the windows overlooking Central Park. The view from those windows was among the best the city had to offer, but at that moment Aimee wouldn't have cared if her living room overlooked a garbage dump swarming with rats. She had a problem. Despite the adage that there is no such thing as bad publicity, being connected to a suspect in a multiple murder was very bad publicity indeed.

"Your brother telephoned," Mildred said in sign language.

"Which one?"

Mildred puffed out her cheeks and drew her hand down her chin, pantomiming a chubby person with a beard, signifying Trainor, the eldest of Aimee's two brothers.

"I was hoping it was the other one," Aimee said.

Under the circumstances, Aimee's other brother, Marsh, would be of far more use than Trainor, who wasn't much smarter than a Labrador retriever. Marsh was an international arms dealer. He was clever and resourceful, with all sorts of contacts in places high and low. If anyone would know how to deal with the current situation, it would be Marsh.

Mildred was aware of the reporters lurking outside, and of why they were there. She'd had the TV on in the kitchen while she was ironing, and had seen a close-captioned report about the bodies discovered in Georgia. Two men, each shot twice in the back of the head, had been discovered on land belonging to a woman named Janet Castleberry. Ms. Castleberry was the former sister-in-law of Blanton Trapnell, who had died not long ago, leaving an estate estimated as being worth a mind-boggling forty billion dollars.

The TV reporter didn't fail to mention that Blanton Trapnell was the father of fashion designer Aimee Trapnell. Her expression as she delivered this information managed to convey both sympathy and unbounded delight. This was big news, as murder connected to the wealthy always is.

Mildred had encountered the scrum of members of the fourth estate hanging around outside the Dakota when she'd gone to pick up Aimee's dry cleaning. She'd passed through them, impervious to their presence, her face blank. That was a good thing about being Deaf; it made it easier to avoid people with whom she preferred not to interact.

"Your brother wants you to call him," she told Aimee.

"I guess I'd better," Aimee said.

"Do you want me to bring you something to drink?"

"Sparkling water with a slice of lime, thanks."

In her youth, Mildred had been a blocker on a women's roller derby team from Long Island called the Mamaroneck Knockers. She'd long since hung up her skates, but she still worked out regularly at a gym. If Aimee had asked her, she wouldn't have hesitated to take off her apron and go downstairs and beat up the reporters. Since Aimee didn't ask that of her, Mildred fetched her employer's drink and went back into the kitchen.

Aimee sank onto a tufted white leather sofa. She took out her mobile phone and called her brother, Trainor. It was answered on the first ring.

"Hello?" piped a child's voice.

Aimee groaned in exasperation. It was her seven-year-old niece, Jubilee. Aimee wasn't fond of Jubilee. She disliked children in general, except for her son, Benjamin, to whom she was devoted. Benjamin was eighteen now, not really a child anymore.

"Jubilee, it's your Aunt Aimee. Put your daddy on the phone."

"Daddy can't talk to you. He's talking to his lawyer," Jubilee said, importantly. "That's because Aunt Yamma's a murderer."

"Yamma is not your aunt," Aimee told Jubilee in a no-nonsense tone. "You have two aunts. Yamma isn't one of them. I'm your aunt. Aunt Karen is your aunt. Yamma is just someone who married one of your Gong-Gong's brothers, a long time ago. After he died, she went and married somebody else. She's not related to you by blood. Only blood relations count, you understand? We call her aunt to be polite, but she's not really part of our family."

Gong-Gong was Jubilee's pet name for her late grandfather, Aimee's father, Blanton. Courtland was the youngest of Blanton's siblings, all of whom were dead now. Courtland had married Janet when he was fifty and she was twenty-three. He always called her Yamma, which was how she'd pronounced her name when she was a toddler. The rest of the family followed suit. The Trapnells were great ones for nicknames. Sometimes it was impossible for outsiders to decipher whom they were talking about.

"But she killed people," Jubilee insisted. "Daddy had to call his lawyer because TV people are outside. Daddy needed to know what to tell them. Is Daddy in trouble?"

"Not this time," Aimee said grimly, thinking of all the times Trainor had been in trouble, usually at the instigation of his friend, Peach Walker.

Peach and his mother operated a moving and storage business based in Mobile, Alabama. While it did some moving and storage, that was only a front for its real business, which was crime. It was said, without much hyperbole, that from Mobile to Gulfport, Mississippi, no stolen goods were fenced, no car was stolen and stripped of its parts, and no drugs were dealt without Peach and his mother getting a cut of the action.

"Mama says we're going to go stay at the condo in Florida, just me and her," Jubilee told Aimee. "Mama says the TV people are getting on her nerves. Mama says she never expected to be married to somebody who got her involved in murder. Mama says…"

Jubilee was interrupted in recounting the things her mother had said by Trainor, who had entered the room, having concluded his consultation with his attorney. Aimee could hear him shouting at Jubilee. "What are you doin' with my phone? I told you a million times not to mess with it."

"But it rang," Jubilee whined.

"I don't care. If it rings, let it alone, you hear? If somebody wants to talk to me and I'm busy, they can leave a message. Don't go answerin' phones. You never know who it might be." He lowered his voice to a hushed, ominous growl. "There are bad people who call little girls on the phone, very, very bad people. When they get a little girl on the phone, they find out where she lives. Then they come to her house at night, stuff her in a dirty, smelly old sack and take her away."

Trainor paused dramatically to that sink in. "I ain't gonna tell you what happens next; it's too awful for a child your age to hear. Let's just say the little girl never sees her mama and daddy again and leave it at that. My point is, if you don't want to get kidnapped and stuffed in a sack, don't answer the phone."

Trainor snatched the phone from Jubilee and spoke into it. "Who's this?"

"It's Aimee," Aimee said. She was impressed by how her normally unimaginative brother was able to plumb a deep well of horror and paranoia in order to frighten his only child. He meant it for Jubilee's own good, but some of his more lurid creations had given the little girl nightmares.

"Jesus, Aimee. Can you believe this shit? There's a flock of news people outside. Yamma had bodies buried on her property. She told the cops she buried them herself. Ain't that the craziest thing you ever heard?" Trainor sounded as if he was about to lose his mind.

"This is bad. We ain't supposed to have news trucks parked outside the house on account of somebody in our family messed around with dead bodies. We ain't that kind of people."

"They're here, too," Aimee told him. "I came back from getting my hair done and there was a mob of them outside. I hate this. It's going to be bad for my brand."

Trainor gave a dismissive snort. "Nobody cares what goes on up in New York City, not folks in Georgia, not ones that matter. They assume it's constant mayhem up there in New York City. It's different in Buckhead. In Buckhead you're only supposed to be in the news because of somethin' good, like if you donated a bunch of money to charity, or because your daughter got picked as the debutante of the year at the Christmas Cotillion. Stuff like that. Positive stuff. Not because your aunt murdered two guys."

Buckhead was the affluent Atlanta neighborhood where Trainor resided in a hideous McMansion, the possession of which he was inordinately proud. Trainor was fortunate in that he was the son of a rich man who had provided him with a generous trust fund. Otherwise, he would probably be living in a bunged-up trailer out in the boondocks somewhere, about to have the electricity shut off for lack of payment.

"Murder makes us look bad. Palmer locked herself in our room. She's cryin' her eyes out. She's afraid this has ruined her chances of gettin' into the Daughters of Arsinoe." Palmer was Trainor's third wife, the mother of Jubilee.

"What's that?"

"It's a club they got down here. Women set great store by it."

"So what if she doesn't get in? Tell her to start her own club. Daddy left us plenty of money. She can start any kind of club she wants."

Trainor vetoed that idea. "It wouldn't have the same whaddya-call-it, cachet, as the Daughters of Arsinoe. That's got history behind it. When the Yankees burned Atlanta, the club ladies linked arms and stood outside the building where they had their meetings. They told the Yankees to go set fire to somethin' else and leave their clubhouse alone. The head Yankee apologized for botherin' them and took his men away. That's history. If Palmer started a club, it wouldn't have that kind of history."

"I guess not," said Aimee. "Does the club still meet in the building they saved from getting burned down by the Yankees?"

"Nope, after the war, it burned down anyway. They got a place in Inman Park now, over by the Krog Street Market." Trainor's voice took on a longing tone. The market was huge, a modern cathedral devoted to the worship of food. Trainor loved to eat. He could happily graze all day, and frequently did. Thinking about the culinary delights of the market's massive food hall made his mouth water.

Tearing his thoughts away from plump, aromatic, pork-filled dumplings and delicious fried chicken, the outside crispy, the inside moist and tender, he continued, "My point is, the Daughters of Arsinoe is a big deal. Palmer's friend, Chandler Woodbury, got in. She's been crowin' about it nonstop, sayin' how nobody counts in Atlanta society unless they're a member. Palmer's desperate to get in. It's all she talks about. It's gettin' on my nerves. If they won't let her join because of this thing with Aunt Yamma I don't even wanna think about what she might do."

Aimee thought he was right about that. Palmer possessed a steely determination to achieve her goals. Once her mind was set on something, she would not be deterred. She was engaged in a longstanding battle for social supremacy with her best friend and arch-enemy, Chandler Woodbury. Chandler had been accepted into the Daughters of Arsinoe. If Palmer's application were rejected, her fury would know no bounds. It might ignite the equivalent of World War III among the wealthy women of Atlanta.

Aimee thought it best to change the subject. "How come you were talking to Dooley?"

Trainor's legal representative was an old college buddy of his named Dooley Voight. A tall, skinny beanpole of a man, Dooley spoke and dressed like a country bumpkin straight out of *Hee Haw.* But appearances were deceiving. Dooley possessed a razor-sharp legal mind. It was said of him by friends and foes alike that he could bail Satan out of Hell.

Dooley had foiled many attempts to bring Peach Walker and his criminal colleagues to justice. When the chips were down, Trainor looked to Dooley to rescue him. So far, he had never failed.

"He called me after he heard the news about Aunt Yamma gettin' caught with dead bodies. He said I needed to issue a statement. He came over and we put one together. He's out front now, talkin' to the reporters. He read 'em the statement."

Aimee was intrigued. Maybe she should get her lawyer to address the media vultures hanging around outside the Dakota.

"What does it say?

"I got a copy here. I'll read it to you." Trainor cleared his throat. "Ahem! As a longtime friend of Trainor Trapnell, one of Atlanta's leading citizens, I felt compelled to speak to you on his behalf. As you know, there has been an unfortunate incident involving a person with a slight connection to Mr. Trapnell's family. We do not yet know the details of what transpired on the property belonging to Ms. Janet Castleberry.

"Mr. Trapnell was shocked to learn that Ms. Castleberry, who at one time, long ago, was briefly married to his uncle, may have been involved in the improper disposal of corpses. The identities of the victims are currently unknown. We do not know what sort of people they were. They may have been good, law-abiding folks. Then again, maybe they weren't.

"I remind you that Ms. Castleberry only claimed to have buried the bodies. She didn't say she killed them. Ms. Castleberry, God bless her, is getting on in years. She may be confused about what happened. She may have been coerced or intimidated.

"In summation, Mr. Trapnell was shocked and saddened by this development involving someone with whom he has a minor family connection. Please respect his privacy. When more is known, I will be happy to speak to you on his behalf. Thank you."

Aimee was impressed. It sounded like Dooley had once again worked his magic. The statement was perfect; it distanced Trainor from his aunt by marriage while at the same time seeming sympathetic to her plight, at least until more was known. If Yamma turned out to be a cold-blooded murderer, Dooley would undoubtedly express outrage on Trainor's behalf.

"That's good. It makes it sound as if Yamma was barely involved with our family, like she was mistake Uncle Courtland made. She was a lot younger than him. Everybody said she got him to marry her by using her feminine wiles. How long were they married? Not long, was it?"

"Fourteen or fifteen years. That's what Palmer says. She's usually right about things like marriages and births and whatnot," Trainor replied.

That was longer than any of Trainor's marriages. It was longer than Aimee had been married to her first husband, or her second. Neither chose to comment on it.

"Maybe this will blow over and we can forget about it," Aimee said.

"I hope so. Palmer's in a state. If this gets her blackballed from the Daughters of Arsinoe I don't want to think about what she'll do. It makes my stomach knot up every time I think about how mad she'll be. She's gotta get in; she's just gotta," Trainor said fervently.

Aimee's phone beeped. Another call was coming in. "Keep me posted on what's happening down there. I'll talk to you later," she told Trainor, and hung up.

The caller was Leighton Knauss. He was supposed to take her to dinner that night at Great Wave, a Michelin-star restaurant on Columbus Circle. An exquisite jewel box of a place, it had seating for only ten guests. Diners paid six hundred dollars apiece to sit at a counter for two hours, watching the chef at work, up close, in what was billed as a genuine *omakase* experience. *Omakase* was a

Japanese phrase used when ordering sushi. It meant, "I leave it up to you."

No one knew ahead of time what they'd be served at Great Wave, but it was said to be unfailingly delicious. Reservations had to be booked months in advance. Aimee had been looking forward to it, but now Leighton was backing out.

"Something came up. I need to take care of it right away. I'll call you," he blurted, and hung up.

Aimee stared at her phone in disbelief. This wasn't like him. Leighton usually wanted to talk for hours once he got her on the phone. Something was wrong. Had he heard about the bodies in Georgia? She had a sinking feeling that he had and was making himself scarce.

At least Avery Panko was still available. He was escorting her to a cocktail party the following night. It was being given by a prominent entertainment attorney at his apartment at the Apthorp.

A massive limestone edifice, built in the Italian Renaissance Revival style, the Apthorp occupied a full city block between Seventy-ninth Street and Broadway. Each of its twelve floors had originally contained ten apartments. Over the years, they had been carved into progressively smaller spaces, renting for progressively higher prices.

The Apthorp was almost as desirable an address as the Dakota. The gathering would be what people in Aimee's social circle called an "important party." The mayor would be there, as well as the woman in charge of the New York Philharmonic's Spring Gala. Also on hand would be a disgraced financier who professed to have found religion while in prison.

This individual had stolen millions of dollars in an audacious Ponzi scheme. He was now a popular guest on TV talk shows. He spoke movingly, tears in his eyes, his voice trembling with emotion, as he expressed remorse for his misdeeds, crediting his newfound relationship with Jesus for bringing about his redemption.

He had established a charitable foundation, ostensibly to benefit the children of prison inmates. Instead, he kept most of the money himself. It was only a matter of time before the law would catch up with him and once again, he would be back in prison, but for now he was enjoying himself.

Aimee's phone rang again, the ringtone playing the opening drumbeats of Beyoncé's "Run the World (Girls)." It was Avery Panko. He was cancelling their date. Something had come up.

Aimee slammed the phone down on the glass-topped coffee table, rattling the ornaments on it. Fists clenched, she fled across the hall, to the apartment where she kept her pets.

CHAPTER THREE
SISTRURUS CATENATUS TERGEMINUS

The apartment across the hall had originally been identical to the one where Aimee lived. She'd purchased it for nine million dollars several years previously. Considerable changes had taken place since then. The parquet floors had been torn out and replaced with tiles in various shades of brown, sculpted to resemble flat rocks.

The original twelve rooms had been reduced to five, leaving a spacious open area containing display cases with glass fronts. The cases had painted backdrops, depicting a desert or a forest or a savannah or a mangrove swamp, depending on their tenant's native habitat. Inside were Aimee's pets. They wound themselves around branches, hid in hollow logs, or stretched out, full-length, beneath heat lamps, absorbing the warmth. Aimee's pets were snakes. She passionately loved them all.

Smaller snakes inhabited terrariums on shelves made of teak, purchased from a company that supplied decking for luxury yachts. The result resembled a state-of-the-art reptile house at a top-notch zoo. Aimee took painstaking care of her pets, assisted by Joaquim Brazos, a herpetologist who had previously worked at the Bronx Zoo.

Aimee paid Joaquim three times what his salary had been at the zoo. She also gave him the use of a suite of rooms at the rear of the apartment where he lived, rent-free. Joaquim worshipped the ground Aimee walked on. Like Mildred Pickering, he would have done anything for her.

Aimee found Joaquim conferring with a deliveryman in a tan uniform. They were examining a snake in a clear plastic box with handles on the sides. The delivery man was short, no more than five feet, four inches tall. He had stringy, shoulder-length blond hair and wore comically large, black-framed, Buddy Holly-style glasses.

"Brung you a snake, missus," the deliveryman said. He grinned at Aimee, displaying horrible brown teeth, marking him as a dedicated chewer of tobacco. "Hit's a good 'un."

"A *sistrurus catenatus tergeminus*," Joaquim added helpfully. "Male, thirty-two inches long."

It was a rattlesnake, light gray, with dark brown blotches. Drop for drop, its venom was more potent than that of many larger species of snake. Its bite could be fatal if left untreated.

"How lovely," said Aimee, her mood brightened by the unexpected arrival of a new snake. She bent down to examine it, her doting expression that of someone admiring an adorable puppy. The snake regarded her with eyes as black and shining as drops of oil. Its tongue flicked, tasting the air.

"Aren't you a handsome boy? Yes, you are," she crooned. Then she remembered that she hadn't ordered any new snakes.

"Where did he come from?" she asked Joaquim.

"Texas," the herpetologist said, glancing at the deliveryman, as if for confirmation.

"That's right," the deliveryman confirmed, pronouncing it *thass rat*. "This here snake come all the way from Texas. Special delivery." He grinned, his appalling teeth suggesting that regular visits to a dentist weren't among his top priorities.

Aimee was confused. "Yes, but why? Who sent him? I didn't order him."

The deliveryman took off his glasses and placed them on top of one of the glass cases. Then he removed his false teeth and blond wig, revealing himself to be none other than Aimee's brother, Marsh.

"He's a gift, from my friend Andy," he said, his educated, dulcet tones replacing the choppy, Appalachian accent he'd used while portraying a deliveryman.

Aimee gasped, "Oh no! Not the one who used to be the president of Ulakistan? Not the lunatic they call the Madman of the Steppes? Please tell me it's not."

"It is," Marsh said cheerfully. He unbuttoned his baggy tan shirt and stepped out of his tan trousers, handing them to Joaquim. Transformation complete, he stood before them in a beautifully tailored suit and starched white shirt, as self-possessed and debonaire as a miniature James Bond.

Aimee put her hands on her hips. She didn't like the sound of this. "Why would Andy, or whatever his real name is, send me a snake?"

"His full name is Andrej Yakov Temirkhan Asgarov Sadyharbaghi That's too much of a mouthful for Americans, so he's calling himself Andy Jacobs now," Marsh said.

Marsh had met the dictator as the result of arms sales he'd made to the Ulakistani military. He had been invited to dine at the Presidential Palace. It was quite a place. The table in the banquet hall was capable of seating one hundred. Blood-red marble columns marched along the sides of the room, each with the circumference of a mighty oak. The high ceiling was decorated with an inaccurate but nonetheless impressive representation of the constellations, done in 14-karat-gold mosaic tiles.

At the first of these formal dinners, the dictator presented Marsh with a dagger, its handle glittering with priceless rubies. In turn, Marsh gave him a plastic cigarette lighter shaped like the Statue of Liberty.

It was a cheap thing, the kind sold at souvenir shops in Times Square. Nevertheless, the despot was enthralled. He kept snapping it open and shut, watching in open-mouthed wonder as the flame appeared and disappeared.

Placing it aside, he sprang from his seat at the head of the table, causing his bodyguards to reach for their guns. Waving them impatiently away, he strode over to Marsh and embraced him. "Thank you for the beautiful gift, Marshov Trapnellovitch," he said.

"I will treasure it forever. From this moment on, you are as a brother to me."

It was, in Marsh's words, "the beginning of a beautiful friendship."

The long-suffering Ulakistanis eventually got fed up with living under the dictator's harsh rule. A band of them stormed the Presidential Palace, baying for blood. Andy managed to escape just in time, fleeing aboard a jet piloted by a military commander who had remained loyal to him. The plane streaked down the runway, its engines roaring full-throttle, while rebels in jeeps gave chase, shouting abuse and firing assault rifles. The plane lifted off, riddled with bullet holes. It turned, dipped a wing, and headed west, out of Ulakistani airspace.

Prior to the coup, Andy had seen which way the wind was blowing. He'd taken the precaution of transferring most of the money in his country's treasury to secret bank accounts in Switzerland and the Caribbean. Now he resided, rich as Croesus, at a ranch in Texas, a guest of the United States government.

What the United State government hadn't bargained for was that Andy wasn't the kind of former head of state who would settle down meekly to life in exile. It wasn't in his nature. Andy wanted payback for the humiliation of being usurped from what he deemed to be his rightful place at the helm of Eastern Europe's smallest nation.

Texas, while initially interesting, came to bore him. Unbeknownst to his protectors, Andy began plotting his escape.

"I doubt you'll ever have occasion to meet him, but if you do, please don't mention that I sold the rebels the rifles they were using to shoot at his plane. I don't think he would take it well," Marsh told Aimee.

"From what you told me about him he'd probably skin you alive."

Aimee had long suspected that Marsh's habit of playing both sides of the fence with his arms deals would eventually prove to be his undoing.

"Rebels—or as they prefer to call themselves, freedom fighters—deserve to be armed, the same as regular fighting forces. It's only fair," Marsh said. "Andy might understand it was nothing personal, but then he might not. He's a little unpredictable. It's best not to bring up anything that might set him off."

"He's called the Madman of the Steppes for a good reason. He's had hundreds of people tortured and killed. He's not 'a little unpredictable;' he's a homicidal maniac," Aimee said.

Turning to the snake in its plastic box, she smiled. "At least he gave me this lovely snake. Let's put him in one of the vacant terrariums where he can stretch out and be comfy. Joaquim, get him settled in his new home."

"Okay," Joaquim said obediently. He lifted the snake in its container and carried it to his workroom.

In its glass case an albino cobra, six feet in length, slowly rose and spread its hood. It swayed from side to side, watching Aimee and Marsh with its sinister red eyes. Around it, other snakes in their cases moved sinuously, thinking their mysterious serpent thoughts.

"Why did your pal Andy give me a snake?' Aimee asked Marsh. He was examining one of the glass-fronted cases, where a huge olive-green snake, thicker than one of his thighs, was draped over a branch.

"Isn't that an anaconda?"

"Yes. What of it?"

"I thought they were illegal in Manhattan."

"They are," his sister replied. "So are ferrets, but that doesn't stop people from owning them."

"Does the co-op board know you've got an anaconda in here?"

"They know I have snakes. To them, all snakes are more or less the same. As long as none of mine escapes they don't have a problem with it, especially since I donated the money to renovate the fountain in the courtyard."

"I see," said Marsh. "Baksheesh, was it?" He was aware of how financial donations— bribes to put it crassly—have a way of making objections disappear.

"Call it what you like. You know, it's strange that you turned up. I just got off the phone with Trainor. He's all upset. The police in Georgia found two bodies buried on land belonging to Aunt Yamma."

Marsh adjusted the platinum links in the cuffs of his Turnbull & Asser shirt. They were engraved with a fouled anchor, a nautical symbol representing the necessity of confronting difficulties and overcoming them, something at which Marsh excelled.

"I heard. As a matter of fact, that's why I'm here. Andy felt terrible about our family being involved in this mess. He considers himself responsible. That's why he wanted you to have that snake. He caught it on the place where he's staying in Texas. I told him how much you like snakes and he said to give it to you, with his compliments. Wasn't that thoughtful of him?"

"I guess so," Aimee said slowly, "but what do you mean he considers himself responsible?" Her voice rose in alarm. "Marsh, what does Andy have to do with those dead bodies?"

He refused to meet her eyes. "Don't get upset."

"Marsh, what happened? Did Andy kill those guys? Did *you* kill them?"

"I have never killed anyone in my life," Marsh said stiffly. "I resent you saying that."

"Bullshit, you've killed lots of people."

"Only in self-defense. Let me remind you that you killed my closest friend, Johnny Rolex, and you tried to murder our stepsister, Karen, so don't get all holier than thou, acting like you're morally superior," Marsh said. Then his tone softened, "Look, I know you had to shoot Johnny or he would have killed us that time in Italy. It's water under the bridge, regrettable but necessary. Trying to kill Karen, though, that was very bad of you. You're lucky she survived and forgave you."

Karen was the daughter of their father and his first wife. She was considerably older than her three step-siblings. She was a Buddhist nun, having formerly run a sweat shop in Nepal which masqueraded as a school for girls. Karen was unusual, as were most of the Trapnells.

Marsh toyed with his cufflinks. "How many people you and I have done away with isn't important right now. Will you listen and let me explain?"

He seated himself in a high-backed rattan chair, its cushions made of bark cloth printed with palm fronds and tropical flowers. They matched the curtains on the windows overlooking the cobblestone courtyard, the centerpiece of which was a circular bronze fountain. It was the one Aimee had paid to have refurbished. The size of a child's wading pool, it was either grand or hideous, depending on one's aesthetic sensibility. A case could be made for it being both.

Marsh threw one leg over the other, straightened the crease in his trousers, and gestured to the rattan chair next to his. The chairs faced the glass-fronted case where the anaconda was slowly lowering itself from the branch into a pool of water. "Andy didn't kill those men, although I believe he was the reason they were there. Have a seat and I'll explain."

Aimee sat. "How come you were in disguise? What was that about?"

"Disguises come in handy. The delivery man one is among my favorites. Nobody looks closely at delivery men. That's how I managed to get past those reporters outside. I called Joaquim and he came down and let me in the service elevator. None of the media people gave me a second glance. Their attention was on the snake in the box. It's misdirection. Magicians do it all the time."

"Why did you say Andy was the reason those bodies were there?"

"It's really kind of funny."

"I don't see anything funny about it," Aimee said. The anaconda had succeeded in lowering itself into the water, leaving only its head sticking out.

"Let me explain. Andy wanted to try computer dating. They don't have anything like it in Ulakistan. Over there, if a man wants to date a woman, he gives her father a goat. If she doesn't have a father, he gives a goat to her eldest brother. If she doesn't have any brothers, he gives her mother a hen and some cheese. It's all very structured. Andy was shocked to find out that's not how we do things here."

Aimee thought about that. "So, if I lived in Ulakistan, Trainor would get a goat from a man who wanted to take me on a date?" She tried to imagine Trainor as a goat famer. She couldn't do it. Goat farming required work. Trainor and work were mutually exclusive.

"Yes, that's how it would go," Marsh confirmed. "Goats formed the basis of the Ulakistani economy for millennia, up until the dawn of the twentieth century. That's when a geologist discovered that Ulakistan has large deposits of manganese ore. As you may know, manganese has many uses, primarily as an industrial alloy."

"I didn't know that. I didn't want to know that," Aimee said, examining her manicured fingernails. "It's boring. Even the word manganese is boring. It makes my brain go numb. Get back to the part about computer dating."

Marsh complied, thinking how, if a subject didn't affect Aimee directly, she had no interest in it. "I told him about the different websites, how you look at people's pictures and post pictures of yourself. I took one of Andy on horseback. It turned out well, if I do say so. He didn't look crazy in it, the way he did in the one I took of him playing with some kittens. That one made him look like the very worst sort of serial killer. He sometimes gets this deranged expression, staring and clenching his teeth in a way that's off-putting. I had to convince him not to wear the bear's head."

"Bear's head?" Aimee echoed, not sure if she'd heard correctly.

"Yes, he has this hollowed-out head of a bear he killed. He claims it was terrorizing some remote village, killing goats and cattle. He says he hunted it down, wrestled it to the ground, and stabbed it to death. There a video of it online, made by one of his aides-de-camp. I can show it to you, if you're interested."

"No thanks," Aimee said. She was intrigued by the idea of a head of state overpowering a bear, but videos could be faked. No doubt this one was. And what kind of person would fight a bear? "What's the deal with the bear's head? You said he wears it?"

"He had a taxidermist preserve the body. It's in the Ulakistani national museum. Everything in the museum relates to Andy in one way or another," Marsh explained. "The head was made into a sort of helmet. Andy brought it with him when he fled Ulakistan. He puts it on and looks out of the eye holes. He thinks it's sexy. Apparently Ulakistani women get off on that sort of thing. I had to tell him that American women probably wouldn't find it attractive."

Aimee grimaced. "He wears a bear's head? That's like something out of a horror movie."

"I don't disagree," said Marsh. "However, you must make allowances for cultural differences. Practices that some cultures find perfectly acceptable are sometimes looked upon with repugnance by other cultures. Andy argued, but in the end, he gave in."

"Smart choice."

Marsh nodded. "We wrote a list of things he likes to do, to add to his profile on the dating websites. I had to talk him out of including some of the things he likes to do. Women generally aren't attracted to men who say their hobbies are forcing their enemies to eat live tarantulas, then stuffing them into the trunk of a hollow tree filled with wasps."

"That would be an automatic swipe left," Aimee said.

Marsh ran a hand over his neatly clipped, dark-brown hair. "Here's where things went awry. The ranch where Andy is currently staying is owned by the federal government. It's closely guarded, located in a no-fly zone. We weren't supposed to use that IP address, for security reasons. Sean really dropped the ball on that one."

In response to Aimee's raised eyebrows, Marsh explained, "Sean was the federal employee whose job it was to keep an eye on Andy's internet activity at the ranch. He's been reassigned to Wengo, Colorado, as a result."

"What's in Wengo, Colorado?"

"Not much," Marsh said. "Wheat farms, grain elevators, a combination convenience store and gasoline station. Sean says there are also two bars, with live music on the weekends. Country in one, rap in the other. That's all there is to relieve the tedium of quotidian existence in Wengo. There's also a Cold War-era missile launch facility. Most of it is underground. Sean works there now, sixty feet below ground, poor fellow." Marsh shook his head in sympathy for the unfortunate IT worker's plight.

"From what Sean told me, it's pretty bleak. Metal walls, concrete floors, buzzing fluorescent lighting, nothing to do but stare at a computer terminal eight hours a day, five days a week, bored to tears that nothing is happening, but terrified that something might. Although on the bright side, the radioactive material was removed, so at least he won't die from radiation poisoning."

"Sounds awful," Aimee said.

"It is, but Sean says it was better than being fired and losing his pension, which is what could have happened. He came this close to getting the axe over the faux pas with Andy's dating profile." Marsh held his thumb and index finger an inch apart to illustrate Sean's narrow escape.

"When we were setting it up, I suggested using the address of Aunt Yamma's vacant property: 1304 Drum Point Road, Blue Ridge, Georgia. That's what we used for the host address inside the IP network. Do you know anything about computers?"

"Not much," Aimee admitted. She knew how to write emails and text messages, and how to scroll around online, looking for things to buy. Other than that, she took little interest in the internet, although she kept track of how her Instagram account was doing. She currently had 200 million followers. Her public relations firm took care of it for her.

"IP stands for Internet Protocol," Marsh explained. "An IP address is assigned to each device connected to a computer network. It basically does two things: network interface identification and location addressing."

Aimee was watching the anaconda and only half listening. This was as boring as a lecture about manganese ore. "So what? How did that IP thing lead to Yamma burying those bodies?"

"I'm getting to that. Sean was supposed to be making sure Andy didn't do anything online that would get him into trouble, or get the government into trouble. He went ahead and used the Drum Point Road address I suggested. He didn't think anyone would be able to find the physical location from the host address. He didn't see why anyone would bother, since Andy was using an assumed name. He didn't think anyone would realize that the guy who posted a picture of himself on a horse, giving his name as Andy Jacobs, used to be the president of Ulakistan.

"Sean screwed up?" Aimee asked.

"Yes, and I hold myself responsible," her brother confessed. "The address on Drum Point Road wasn't listed along with Andy's profile on the dating websites. That was supposed to be kept private, known only to the companies that run the sites. Andy's profile would simply say he was from Georgia. My rationale in using that address was that nobody lived there, so what harm could it do? Plenty, as it turned out."

"I'll say," Aimee said, thinking of the clamoring reporters outside the Dakota.

"In hindsight, I should have known better," Marsh admitted. "I don't know why I thought of the Drum Point Road address; it just came into my head. Yamma took me there one time. I didn't even know if I remembered it correctly, but it appears I did, because two men who intended to assassinate Andy turned up there, expecting to find him, and instead somebody killed them."

"Wait! Those two dead guys were after Andy?"

"It looks that way."

"Couldn't it have been a coincidence? Couldn't they have been killed for some other reason, one that had nothing to do with Andy? Criminals murder each other all the time."

Marsh had wondered the same thing initially, but he quickly discounted the idea. No, Andy had to have been the intended target. Blue Ridge was the type of small town which is often described as quaint, or idyllic. People go there to ride the Blue Ridge Scenic Railway, or to take in a play or a concert, or to visit the boutiques, breweries, and restaurants. It's not the kind of place where bodies commonly turn up, shot in the head, gangland-style.

Aimee mused, "A hacker could do that, get the address, I mean."

"Apparently one did. It must have given the feds a scare. Here they thought they had Andy buttoned up, safe and sound, on a ranch in Texas, out in the middle of nowhere. It's guarded day and night, with top-of-the-line surveillance equipment, guard dogs, armed security personnel, the works. Planes aren't even allowed to fly over it, that's how secure it is. Then, against all odds, he was identified through a photo on a dating website. What are the chances of that happening?" Marsh threw up his hands and laughed ruefully.

"Those dating sites have thousands of photos on them. Someone must have used facial recognition software to go through all of them, on the off-chance that Andy's picture was there. Then they sent two hitmen to Aunt Yamma's property, and somebody killed *them*. If Andy had been there, he would have been toast."

"Someone must be determined to kill him, to go to all that trouble," Aimee mused. "You know what this reminds me of? Your other friend, Princess Farah, the heir to the throne of Ishran. You said she lives in a compound in Iceland, protected by armed guards, because the radicals who overthrew her father's government and killed her entire family are out to get her, too."

"The same thought crossed my mind. Poor Princess Farah! She's a marvelous hostess, very considerate of her guests' comfort. One time when I was visiting her, she knitted me a pair of socks; that's what a nice person she is. I told her my feet were chilly and the next day she presented me with a pair of warm socks, which she sat up all night to knit."

Aimee was unimpressed. "She probably didn't have anything better to do."

"A nice woman like that shouldn't have to live like a hunted animal simply because her father's regime was oppressive and cruel, as were his father's, and *his* father's, all the way back for hundreds of years," Marsh said.

Aimee couldn't have cared less about the political situation in Ishran. There were no Clobber boutiques there, due to it being under the control of religious fanatics who would have had heart attacks if Ishrani women appeared in public wearing the kind of clothing Aimee designed. "What I don't understand is why Yamma buried those bodies. Why didn't she call the police?"

"We can ask her that ourselves," Marsh said. "She's about to be released on bail. We should go to Georgia right away and talk to her. It would be better than you staying here, under siege by those savages from the media. There's nothing keeping you here, is there?"

"Not a thing." Once the news broke about the dead bodies, her two suitors, once so eager for her company, had deserted like rats fleeing a sinking ship. It didn't seem likely that they'd be back anytime soon.

Marsh consulted his Audemars Piguet 18-karat white gold Royal Oak, one of a dozen ultra-high-end timepieces he owned. "A plane's leaving in exactly fifty-three minutes. Say goodbye to your snakes. Call your driver. Tell him to take us to the airport and don't spare the horses."

CHAPTER FOUR
THE FBI CAN DO WHATEVER IT WANTS

The news crews outside the Dakota paid no attention as a delivery man exited the building. Neither did they do more than glance at the two women who left a few minutes later. One of them, the taller one, wore dark glasses and a NY Yankees baseball cap with the bill pulled down low. She pushed a collapsible cart on wheels, the kind city-dwellers use when going grocery shopping. Her companion had a lumpy canvas laundry bag slung over one shoulder. Both wore knit slacks and cheap cotton blouses. The news people turned away, uninterested in two dowdily dressed women, obviously servants of some kind.

Baby Patty Cake faced the cameras, having seized the opportunity to promote her latest album. She was vigorously chewing gum while talking to Leticia Guerrero, the reporter from News 3 New York. A large man with a thick gold chain encircling his neck stood protectively beside the pink-haired rapper, his muscular arms folded across his massive chest.

"Aimee and me are close, ya know? Just this morning she was at my crib, listening to tracks from my new album, *All Y'all Be Hos.* It drops in three days. Everybody says it's my best work so far," Baby Patty Cake told Leticia Guerrero, who nodded encouragingly.

The truth was Baby Patty Cake hadn't spoken to Aimee since their encounter in the elevator. That didn't deter her from inserting herself into this drama involving corpses in Georgia. Baby Patty Cake hadn't gotten to where she was by being reticent.

"Did she just say we were all hos?" one of the reporters asked the one standing next to him.

"I think it's the name of her new album," the other reporter replied. The first reporter shook his head, uncomprehending. His favorite song was "Happy," by Pharrell Williams. It made him feel happy. Pharrell Williams didn't sing about hos.

"What was her last album called? Something weird, wasn't it?"

"THOT."

"Thought?"

"No, *THOT.* It's an acronym; it stands for That Ho Over There."

"Which ho?"

"No particular one; it's a derogatory term that means…" The reporter trailed off, confused. He was finding it difficult to keep up with the jargon used by young people. "Just hos in general. It's not meant for any specific ho."

He was wrong about that. *THOT,* the album, was a diss directed at another rapper, whose legal name was Donna Cronk, but who, for professional purposes, called herself Platinum Champagne. A lively feud had sprung up between Baby Patty Cake (the former Jarvenette McNeil) and Platinum Champagne, making headlines and bolstering both their careers.

Baby Patty Cake leaned closer to Leticia Guerrero's microphone. "Aimee swore me to secrecy, so I can't say much, but this thing down in Georgia? My girl Aimee said it's got serious implications." She nodded solemnly upon delivering this whopper of a lie. "It goes all the way up to the highest levels of government, and beyond. Word is, the Illuminati are involved."

Leticia Guerrero, seasoned newswoman that she was, didn't even blink. "Thank you, Baby Patty Cake. Now let's go to Ricky Lippman in the News Three studio to find out what the weekend's weather has in store for us."

Waiting on the other side of Central Park was a gunmetal gray Lincoln Navigator, its engine running, its windows tinted black. Aimee got in the back while Mildred Pickering placed the laundry bag in the trunk. That duty accomplished, the housekeeper retreated into the park, trundling the shopping cart as she retraced her steps to the Dakota.

The Lincoln pulled out into traffic. It headed along the Henry Hudson Parkway, a uniformed driver at the wheel.

Aimee groused, "I wish I could change clothes. I don't like wearing these things of Mildred's. I'm afraid someone will see me in them. Can't we pull over somewhere?"

"We've no time," Marsh replied. He had wriggled out of his deliveryman disguise while waiting for his sister and was once again his usual meticulously attired self. "We mustn't delay. We have a flight to make."

Aimee looked out of the window as they sped past billboards advertising immigration lawyers and dental implants and places offering to pay cash for gold. To the right was a concrete barrier spray-painted with graffiti. The road dipped as they entered a tunnel. Aimee turned to her brother in panic. "This isn't the way to Kennedy, or LaGuardia. It's the lower level of the George Washington Bridge! Don't tell me we're leaving from Newark Airport. I hate that airport. The last time I was there one of those horrible TSA people was rude to me."

"Relax, we're not leaving from Newark. We're leaving from Teterboro."

"Why?"

Marsh's satisfied smile made him resemble the Cheshire Cat. "I wanted it to be a surprise when we got there, but I'll tell you now. It's where I keep my plane."

That was news to Aimee. "Since when have you owned a plane?"

"Since I inherited ten billion dollars from Daddy. It's a good plane, too. All the sultans and oligarchs have ones like it. And I have another surprise. A mystery guest will be joining us."

Traffic was light. It took less than thirty minutes to reach Teterboro Airport, in Bergen County, New Jersey. The entire way, Aimee badgered her brother, trying to lean the identity of the mystery guest. He refused to tell her, saying only, "You'll be surprised. Wait and see."

At the airport, they pulled up in front of the private terminal. The driver went around and opened the rear door for Aimee and Marsh to disembark. Then he removed the laundry bag from the trunk. He opened the door of the terminal and handed the bag to Aimee. Wishing them a safe journey he touched his cap and drove away.

"What do you think of this? I know how much you like your creature comforts," Marsh said, gesturing to the terminal's airy interior. The ceiling was paneled in varnished wood, creating a warm, welcoming feeling. Scattered here and there on the stone floor were area rugs the color of oatmeal, around which comfortable chairs and sofas were grouped. Aside from a woman behind a high-top counter, who was unpacking a carton of bottled water, there was no one in sight.

"You're making it sound like I'm spoiled," said Aimee, who was thoroughly spoiled. "You like nice places, too."

"True, however, unlike you, I'm capable of roughing it, should the need arise," her brother said. "I once spent eight days trapped in a cave in the mountains of Slovenia. My sojourn there was not pleasant. It was cold and damp, as caves often are. I was forced to eat bugs. I won't mention what I drank. You wouldn't survive a single day in a cave."

"That's because I wouldn't have to," Aimee told him. "It was probably your own fault. You're always getting mixed up with people who are out to get you. If you had a respectable profession, you wouldn't have to eat bugs in a cave."

Then the terminal's posh surroundings got the better of her. "This is a nice place," she admitted, looking around with pleasure. "It's not crowded, the way big airline terminals are. I hate it when they make you to stand in line with strangers, and force you take your shoes off. They shout at you if you don't do it fast enough."

"No standing in line here," Marsh assured her. "No taking your shoes off, either. They don't care what I bring on board my plane.

I've brought things with me when I departed from Teterboro that would have gotten me hustled into a little room at one of the major airports and grilled for hours by officious flunkies from the Homeland Security Agency. They're more relaxed here, respectful of people's privacy."

Aimee could only imagine what sort of things her brother might have brought with him on his flights out of Teterboro. Firearms, certainly. Dynamite? Wild animals? Foods that weren't permitted in the United States, like casu marzu, a cheese made in Sardinia, filled with wiggling maggots? There was a market for forbidden foodstuffs among wealthy gourmands. With Marsh, anything was possible.

"Why don't you go over to that restroom and change into your own clothes? It will make you feel better." Marsh indicated floor-to-ceiling windows overlooking the airport's runways. "I'll meet you over by those windows."

Once again dressed in her own clothes, Aimee found Marsh seated on a leather sofa, a tiny cup and saucer balanced on one impeccably tailored knee. Standing over him was an athletic-looking woman. Her makeup was confined to the barest hint of blush on her high cheekbones. Her hair, black as a crow's wing, was scraped into a bun at the nape of her neck. Her deliberately austere appearance failed to detract from the fact that she resembled a young goddess.

The woman's jacket and trousers were black, as were her low-heeled shoes, which were polished to a high gloss. She had a buttoned-up, squared-away demeanor that hinted at an affiliation with the military, or law enforcement.

She was clearly unhappy to be there.

Marsh rose and placed his hand on the woman's arm. She shrugged him off. Unbothered, Marsh told Aimee, "Look who's here! It's my very own Woman in Black, Special Agent Carson Burns. Agent Burns, as you may recall, is a source of unceasing pride and delight to the Federal Bureau of Investigation."

The two women had met before, when Marsh foiled an attempt by a group of fanatics to cause a volcano to erupt, in hope of bringing about the end of the world.

Agent Burns nodded to Aimee, before turning to Marsh with a frown. "I am not your Woman in Black, Bad Choices. Don't ever get the idea that I like you, because I don't."

Burns was Marsh's "handler." He had made a deal with the FBI to provide it with information from time to time in return for immunity from prosecution for escapades that more than likely would have put him behind bars for the rest of his life. Bad Choices was Marsh's code name. Carson Burns had suggested it, considering it apt, having read his file. It ran to more than a thousand pages. As far as she was concerned, Marsh's entire life consisted of a series of bad choices.

Marsh sat down and smiled roguishly at her. "Cheer up, Agent Burns. Remember how we met? Wasn't that fun?"

Burns' frown deepened. "It was not fun. You almost got us both killed. Who the hell buys a submarine at an auction of used military hardware and sells it to a Nicaraguan drug lord? Why the hell did you do that?"

Marsh chuckled, as if amused by the memory. "I was surprised to learn he was a drug lord and that he intended to smuggle drugs in it. He told me he was an oceanographer, like Jacques Cousteau. He said he needed a submarine in order to study endangered fish."

"Bullshit," scoffed Burns.

"No, really! I had no idea," Marsh said, his handsome gray eyes open wide, as if he was incredulous that Burns didn't believe him. "Who am I to deny a man a submarine when he has the means to pay for one? Especially when he spoke so movingly about his lifelong dream of saving the ruffle-gilled grunion from extinction. How could I stand in his way after hearing that?"

"There's no such thing as a ruffle-gilled grunion," the FBI agent told him.

"I know that now. I didn't then," Marsh said.

"You're lying," Burns snapped. "You knew. You're not stupid. You knew what he was up to."

"At the time, I was ignorant of his true purpose," Marsh said. "It's true that his crew had a large arsenal of firearms, more than one would expect oceanographers to have, but until they forced us to get on board and announced the intention of killing us, I dismissed it as simply a harmless quirk."

Burns snorted in disgust. "You're such a liar. Listen, I'm assigned to keep an eye on you. That doesn't mean I'm happy about it. You're a menace to society. I'd rather keep an eye on a cannibal, or a bank robber, or a cannibal who dabbles in bank robbery."

"I saved the world once. That should count for something." Marsh held his espresso cup daintily between thumb and forefinger and swallowed the contents in a single gulp, Italian-style.

"That was pure luck on your part. If that suitcase bomb had gone off, we'd be dead, along with all higher forms of life on Earth," Burns said.

Marsh gave a nonchalant shrug. "But we didn't die. All's well that ends well." Turning to Aimee, he explained, "That's the title of a play, a comedy by William Shakespeare. He was a famous writer. Perhaps you've heard of him."

Aimee wasn't taking the bait. "Everybody's heard of him. Don't think you're some kind of brainiac because you can quote one of his plays. Big deal."

"Ouch, that stings. Agent Burns, my sister is being mean to me. I wish to make a complaint."

Burns sighed, having grown tired of the unrepentant Marsh. She asked Aimee, "How have you been?"

"I'm all right. Marsh said a mystery guest would be joining us. I guess you're it."

"Nope," said a voice, "I'm it."

It was Aimee's son, Benjamin. His curly black hair stuck up in wild tufts and he had a crazed gleam in his eyes. In one hand he clutched a cardboard cup of coffee. In the other was a box of chocolate-chip cookies.

"This is so cool," he enthused. "Agent Burns came to my school. She showed her ID and got me out. The FBI can do whatever it wants. Her car's got a light that flashes red and blue. It's got a siren, too. She showed me how it works in the parking lot, before we left school. She could have driven us here at one hundred and twenty miles an hour if she wanted to, siren wailing, lights flashing, making everybody get out of the way, but she didn't. She didn't even hit the lights and siren; she drove like a regular person who doesn't have the right to drive fast."

He looked downcast for a moment over having missed out on the thrilling experience of rocketing along at more than twice the legal speed limit, but then he brightened. "They have free coffee here! Really good coffee! I had three cups so far. See these cookies?" He shook the box, making it rattle. "They let you take as many as you want."

His boarding school didn't allow its charges to drink coffee. The unaccustomed caffeine had gone to his head.

Aimee hugged him, taking care not to spill his coffee. "You have almost another month left before school's out for the summer. What about your grades?"

"My grades are fine. Straight A's, in fact. I finished all my assignments early and was just waiting for the semester to be over. The headmaster didn't mind me leaving. Ever since I saved the school from getting burned down by that crazy groundskeeper, they can't do enough for me. They'd probably make me the headmaster, if I asked them to."

"That's an exaggeration," Burns said. "And just to be clear, the FBI can't do whatever it wants."

"Yeah, sure," Benjamin laughed, not believing it for one second.

Agent Burns' father, Cleveland Burns, was the first Black student ever admitted to Rayburn Academy, a boarding school for boys in Pennsylvania's Allegheny Mountains. Rayburn, like Exeter and

Choate, acted as a conduit to the universities of the Ivy League. What followed, it was tacitly understood, would be a lifetime of glittering success.

Cleveland Burns went on to become a professor of political science at Georgetown University and an assistant secretary of state. He was one of Rayburn's most distinguished alumni and the reason why Benjamin was admitted. Agent Burns had prevailed upon her father to take a gamble on Marsh's wayward nephew and plead his case to the director of admissions.

The gamble paid off. Benjamin went from being an unruly teen who had dropped out of school to live among street kids, taking drugs and getting into trouble, to being a model student. Earlier that year he had thwarted an arsonist by shooting him with a potato gun. The school's administration was fervently grateful. They'd named the new field house after him, the arsonist having burned down the old one. The yearbook, a volume called *Whispers,* in which the mischievous student staff did its best to sneak double-entendres past the harried English teacher who was its advisor, had been dedicated to Benjamin. If he wanted to leave three weeks early, he could do so.

Marsh looked out the window. "Here comes our plane."

Aimee wasn't impressed by the sight of the little Beechcraft Skipper rolling toward the building. "That plane doesn't look big enough to hold all four of us. I thought you said you owned a jet, like the ones oil-rich sheikhs have. I'm surprised at you, Marsh. If I knew you intended us to fly to Georgia in a puddle jumper, I would have chartered something more suitable."

At that moment an enormous teal-blue aircraft, an erupting volcano painted on its tail, moved majestically past the Beechcraft, dwarfing it the way the *Queen Elizabeth II* would a dinghy. It came to a stop next to the terminal. A set of steps were lowered and two cabin attendants in smart dove-gray uniforms descended.

"That's my plane," said Marsh smugly. "She's called the *Pele*, after the Hawaiian volcano goddess. It's a tribute to my significant other,

Dr. Hannah Ryczak. As you may recall, Dr. Ryczak is one of the world's foremost volcanologists."

He bowed to his speechless companions. "Ladies, Benjamin, if you're ready, let's get on board. Georgia, here we come!"

CHAPTER FIVE
DOOLEY EARNS HIS FEE

They practically had to pry Benjamin out of the *Pele* upon their arrival at Southwest Georgia Regional Airport. He was grinning from ear to ear, almost delirious with excitement.

"I love this plane. It's got everything!" he said. "There are bedrooms back there, and a dining room and a kitchen with a man in a chef's hat in it. He made me the best grilled-cheese sandwich I ever ate. There's a media center, with flat-screen TVs and hundreds of movies on Blu-ray, including the director's cut of *Ishi-Naka-Gira, Underwater Monster Girl.* It's my favorite movie in the entire world."

"You'll notice it has that new-plane smell," Marsh said proudly.

"I love the new-plane smell," Benjamin enthused. "I love everything about this. Can't we fly around a little longer? Please? There's plenty of fuel. I asked one of the cabin attendants and she said it carries enough fuel to fly from New York to Sydney, Australia, nonstop. Let's go to Las Vegas, what do you say?"

"I say viva Las Vegas, just not today," Marsh said. "Dooley Voight, your Uncle Trainor's lawyer, is meeting us. He's going to drive us to White Oaks. Aunt Yamma will be staying there. Dooley paid her bail this morning."

White Oaks was a plantation house in South Georgia, the ancestral home of the Trapnell family.

"She's at White Oaks? How come? Doesn't she have her own house to go to?" Aimee threw aside the cashmere blanket on her lap and sulked. Like Benjamin, she had been dazzled by the plane's plush carpeting, buttery leather seats and shining mahogany trim, but now her enjoyment was replaced by indignation that Yamma would be staying with them. She had hoped to avoid the old lady, whose unauthorized burial of corpses had spoiled Aimee's romantic life.

Agent Burns spoke up. "It was decided that Ms. Castleberry would be safer at White Oaks."

"Safer from what?"

"From whoever killed those men."

"Why would they bother with a batty old lady?"

"We don't know, but it was decided it was best to have all of you together in one place, with me keeping an eye on things, just in case."

Glancing disapprovingly at Marsh, Burns added, "It wasn't my idea. I work out of the Atlanta field office now. Since I'm already acquainted with your family, in particular with you, Bad Choices, I was the one chosen for this gig. Lucky me."

Agent Burns had previously been assigned to the FBI's Bozeman, Montana field office. Atlanta was a huge step up. Being assigned to Atlanta was a coveted career move in the bureau. Burns was grateful to have been given the opportunity, but she was aware that it came at a heavy price, namely that of being in proximity to Marsh Trapnell.

"He's awful," she had complained to her immediate boss, Special Supervisory Agent Ronald DiFranco.

"I'm aware of that, Agent Burns," DiFranco assured her. "I've met the son of a bitch."

He snorted in disgust. "Graduated first in his class from Harvard, every opportunity in the world open to him, and what does he do? Becomes a goddamn arms dealer."

DiFranco was a product of the College of New Jersey, having graduated without distinction, somewhere in the middle of his class. Tall, broad-shouldered, peering at the world through suspicious brown eyes beneath a prominent brow ridge, he was the epitome of an old-school G-man.

DiFranco would have given his eyeteeth to have gone to Harvard. He fancied that if he had, he would be a senator by now. If he had graduated from Harvard, or from any of the Ivies, he'd downplay it when someone asked where he'd gone to school. Cool and nonchalant, he'd drop the name casually, as if it didn't matter. Instead, he felt a burning sense of shame every time he was forced to acknowledge the College of New Jersey as his alma mater. Who graduates from there, anyway? Nobody worth mentioning.

Annoyed, DiFranco fussed with the pens on his desk, aligning them next to a framed photograph of his wife. "We have to deal with people like Marsh Trapnell, Agent Burns; it's part of the job."

"There are no other people like Marsh Trapnell," she replied, quickly adding, "sir," when he gave her a peevish look. He nodded in reluctant agreement.

"Too smart for his own goddammed good. He's a slick little bastard, with his custom-made suits, and the way he travels all over, hobnobbing with royalty." The thought of Marsh's glamorous lifestyle caused a vein in DiFranco's forehead to throb. He forced himself to unclench his jaw. He tended to grind his teeth. For that reason, he wore a night guard, but he couldn't very well wear it at work. He took a deep, calming breath, inhaling through his nose, and holding it to a count of five before slowly exhaling through his mouth, the way his therapist had taught him.

Envy played a large part in DiFranco's attitude toward Marsh, whose suits and footwear were made expressly for him on London's Savile Row. DiFranco's suits came from off the rack at T.J. Maxx. It was also where he bought his shoes. No hand-sewn leather footwear for him, crafted using a pair of wooden lasts specially made to conform to the unique contour of his feet, the way Marsh's shoes were.

DiFranco's thoughts never strayed far from Marsh Trapnell. In that respect he was like a certain ship's captain who became obsessed with a white whale. DiFranco knew, for example, that Marsh was friends with a fabulously wealthy princess who lived, hermitlike, in a fortified compound in Iceland. He was painfully aware that Marsh's picture appeared regularly in the gossip magazines, escorting duchesses and baronesses to polo matches and charity balls. Marsh also had some sort of connection to a woman named Ryczak, who did something involving volcanoes. She had been awarded a Vetlesen Prize, which DiFranco understood to be a sort of Nobel Prize for the Earth sciences.

The most important woman DiFranco had ever met was a Supreme Court justice. They were seated at the same table at a dinner one time. He couldn't claim they were friends. She probably had no idea who he was. The women Marsh associated with clearly knew who *he* was. Judging by the photographs, they were overjoyed to be in his presence. That a reprobate like Marsh Trapnell existed, rich, handsome, popular, floating serene and cloudlike above the world of honest citizens and ordinary criminals infuriated DiFranco.

In his opinion, Marsh was no better than any other snitch the bureau was running, no better than some impetigo-encrusted scumbag who had been caught operating a meth lab in the backwoods of Arkansas. It was too bad that Marsh had found favor with the director, DiFranco thought sourly.

DiFranco consoled himself with the thought that FBI directors come and go. With luck, the next one might be amenable to coming down hard on Mr. Fancypants Trapnell.

"I understand your sentiments, Agent Burns, I truly do, but..." DiFranco stood, indicating the meeting was over. "Into each life some rain must fall, eh? And you'll get to stay at White Oaks. I've heard it's quite a place. Acres of perfectly tended gardens. Architecturally stunning. Southern hospitality at its finest. You'll enjoy it, I'm sure. Keep me posted. Stick to Marsh Trapnell like glue. I want to know every move he makes."

Burns was brought out of her reverie by Aimee asking, "You said, 'it was decided.' Who decided?" Aimee was frustrated by Burns' opaque way of speaking. "Don't we get any say in it?"

"It was the FBI," Benjamin said, nodding sagely. "The FBI can do whatever it wants."

"You keep saying that. Don't say that; it's not true," Burns told him. "It was another government agency." DiFranco had told her that much, before clamming up. "You've never heard of it. Hardly anyone has heard of it. If you're lucky you never will hear of it. It just so happens that it *can* do whatever it wants. If it tells the FBI to jump, it does, no questions asked. Don't blame me. I'm only the babysitter here."

"Covert ops. Dark money. Activities so secret even the president doesn't know about them," Benjamin said admiringly. Burns remained silent and outwardly impassive, although inwardly, she was surprised by how accurate his guess was.

"What offense was Yamma charged with?" Marsh asked.

"A fairly minor one, as it turned out. There was no evidence that she killed anyone. She told the police she discovered two dead bodies on her property when she went there to tend her husband's grave. She said she thought it best to bury them herself, on the spot."

Benjamin gave a delighted laugh. Like many teenagers, he had a love of the macabre. "That's crazy. It's like something out of Edgar Allan Poe, or what was that story, the one about the lady who kept her dead boyfriend in her bed?"

"It's 'A Rose for Emily,' by William Faulkner," Burns said. "What Ms. Castleberry did was nowhere near as bad, although it was certainly unusual. Under Georgia law there's nothing to prohibit what's known as home burial. Local zoning law allowed Ms. Castleberry to inter her husband's ashes on private land, which she holds the title to. Under the same zoning law, it would theoretically be all right for her to allow other burials there. Where she ran into trouble was in failing to notify the police that a crime had been committed. Initially, she faced additional charges of two counts of abandonment of a dead body. That's a felony, punishable with prison time. Mr. Voight managed to convince them to only charge her with failing to notify the police."

Aimee snickered, seeing it as proof that Yamma was crazy. "What kind of person finds two dead bodies and doesn't tell the police?"

Burns shrugged. "People sometimes do funny things. A ranger from the national park happened to be driving by and noticed someone working in the field, wearing a headlamp. He went to see if he could be of assistance. That's when he saw it."

"The dead bodies?" Benjamin asked.

"One dead body," Burns said, holding up her index finger. "Male Caucasian, age approximately thirty to forty. The body was at the bottom of a freshly dug grave. Ms. Castleberry was in the process of shoveling dirt over it. The ranger called the police. It wasn't clear at first whether it was federal land, since it borders on a national park, so the FBI was called in. Subsequent examination of the area revealed another freshly dug grave. It contained another body, with the same general description as the first."

"That is so crazy," Benjamin said, visibly thrilled. "Aunt Yamma was wearing a headlamp? The kind cave explorers wear?"

"They're called spelunkers," Marsh told his nephew. "It makes sense to wear a headlamp if one is going to be digging after dark in an isolated area."

"Is that what you do? Wear a headlamp when you bury bodies after dark?" Benjamin was aware that his uncle had been stabbed a few times in the course of his work, and had been shot on occasion. Marsh was not the sort to let violent assaults on his person go without retaliating. Benjamin suspected his uncle had dug a few graves in his time, either that or he made other people dig them, the same people who were about to be interred in them.

"That's not germane to the current situation," Marsh coolly replied.

Benjamin asked Agent Burns, "When you said it wasn't that bad for her to be burying those guys, how did you know? How do you know if it was legal or not?"

"That's what the agent at the scene told me. I double-checked on the legality. I have a degree from Columbia Law School. FBI agents often have law degrees," Burns told him.

Benjamin considered that, his head to one side. "I used to think I'd like to be a defense contractor, like Uncle Marsh. Now I'm starting to wonder if the FBI wouldn't be a good career to go into. You get to find out things nobody else knows, and you get to boss people around and tell them what to do. They have to do what you say, or else you send them to prison."

"That's not how it works," Burns said. Seeing Benjamin was unconvinced, she gave up. "Let's go meet Mr. Voight. He can fill us in on what he learned from the police."

"I must say, I'm disappointed in you," Marsh told Benjamin as the plane taxied to a stop. "I was pleased when you expressed an interest in joining me in my business. It saddens me to hear you've been bewitched by the tawdry lure of a gold badge and the authority it bestows upon its holder to harass the citizenry." He sighed theatrically. "Oh well, you're still young. There's plenty of time for you to change your mind. Trust me, you don't want to be stuck plodding along on the dreary treadmill of civil service, your every move dictated by the whims of incompetent political appointees."

Burns chuckled. "Give me a break. You sell tanks and fighter planes to whoever pays you the most money. You have the ethics of a sewer rat. You're in no position to give career advice."

"On the contrary, my business is eminently respectable," Marsh said, causing Burns to laugh harder.

"Bad Choices, you're a piece of work," she said.

Dooley Voight drove them the thirty-five miles from the airport to Cobbs, a sleepy village not far from the Florida border. Cobbs had been the domain of the Trapnell family for generations. On the outskirts of town was their plantation house, White Oaks. It sprawled, vast and palatial under the late afternoon sun, its meticulously tended green lawns, columned portico and dazzling white façade a vision of opulence.

Holy cow, thought Burns, stunned by the sight. *It's a genuine Georgia plantation. Leave it to Bad Choices to own a plantation.*

As if he had read her mind, Marsh said, "A penny for your thoughts, Agent Burns."

"My thoughts aren't worth a penny," she replied.

"I sincerely doubt that. I'll show you around later. There are many interesting things to see at White Oaks. There's a graveyard that's supposed to be haunted, and a room where one of my ancestors kept his wife imprisoned for twenty years. The story goes that it stemmed from them having a disagreement over a game of whist. The scratches are still visible on the back of the door, where she clawed at it in a futile attempt to escape."

"Great," said Burns. "Can't wait to see that."

"I sure do enjoy comin' out here to y'all's stately home," Dooley said to Marsh, as he piloted his Lexus up the mile-long drive paved with white oyster shells. The shells crunched beneath the car's tires, as it rolled along at a sedate five miles per hour.

Dooley had the air-conditioning turned up. The thermometer on the dashboard registered eighty-eight degrees Fahrenheit. That was considered normal, even a bit cool, for Cobbs in late May. It would be another month before the real heat would set in, causing all outdoor activity to grind to a torpid, tropical crawl.

Aimee was already having reservations about returning to her ancestral home. The last time she was there, she and Marsh and Trainor, as well as their stepsister, Karen, had almost been murdered. The time before that, Trainor had allowed their father to strangle a sideshow performer. Bad things had a way of happening at White Oaks.

Aimee resolved to watch her back. She hoped the level-headed presence of Special Agent Burns would be a calming influence.

"This is the second time today I been here," Dooley remarked as they approached the circular turnaround in front of the house. In the center, a marble fountain in the shape of a pod of dolphins sent jets of water into the air.

Pulled up to the portico steps was Blanton's white 1959 Rolls-Royce Silver Wraith. Its tall, stainless-steel radiator grille was topped by a sculpture of a crouching woman, her robes billowing out behind her. "Nellie in her Nightie," was how jocular Rolls-Royce factory workers used to refer to the mascot, although its official name was the Spirit of Ecstasy. Parked behind the Rolls was a cherry-red BMW XM sedan.

"I drove Miz Castleberry here from Blue Ridge after I paid her bail this mornin'. Took me nearly five hours," Dooley said, pulling in behind the BMW. "Then I went to pick y'all up at the airport. Now I'm back. That's another two hours, near about." He turned off the ignition and massaged the back of his neck. "I been busy as a one-legged man in an ass-kicking contest."

Then he remembered there were ladies present. "Pardon my language," he apologized to Aimee and Agent Burns. "It's been a long day. I forgot myself."

"We appreciate your efforts," Marsh told him. "Please submit a bill for your time."

"Don't worry, I will," the lawyer said. Puzzled, he gazed up at the enormous mansion looming above them. "I swear, this big ol' house got bigger since this morning."

"It does that," Aimee said matter-of-factly. "Sometimes it grows overnight, when no one is looking."

Dooley wasn't sure whether she was joking. Marsh and Benjamin gave no indication of what they thought about her remark. *Maybe she means it,* the lawyer thought uneasily.

"I believe that BMW belongs to Trainor. He and Palmer are probably inside with Yamma," Marsh said as he stepped out of the car, into the stultifying heat and a whir of insects. Unruffled, he went around to open the car door for his sister and Agent Burns.

CHAPTER SIX
WALK RIGHT IN

Aimee passed through the portico with its towering Corinthian columns and entered the house, followed by Marsh and Benjamin and Dooley Voight. Agent Burns brought up the rear. The heavy oak door swung shut behind them with a genteel thud. The delicately carved fanlight above it threw pie-shaped wedges of sunlight onto a vast expanse of gleaming black-and-white checkerboard marble floor.

The heat and humidity had made even the short walk from the car to the house uncomfortable. Agent Burns breathed a sigh of relief at the cool air circulated by the central air-conditioning. It had been installed at tremendous expense on orders from Blanton Trapnell's second wife, the mother of Marsh, Trainor, and Aimee. The late Deidre Trapnell was from Rochester, New York, and could not abide the oppressive heat of southern Georgia.

Burns couldn't imagine what it must cost to air-condition a house this size. She looked around the cavernous entry hall, craning her neck to take in the high ceiling, where a huge, glittering crystal chandelier hung suspended on a golden chain. She was intrigued despite herself by being inside Marsh's boyhood home.

Then she realized something.

"You walked right in," she told Aimee.

"Why not? White Oaks is part mine." Aimee put the laundry bag containing Mildred's clothes and a few things of her own on the floor, next to a French Second Empire table. It was an outré object, its gilded, curved columns shaped like bare-breasted women wearing Egyptian headdresses.

Above them rose a double-reverse spiral staircase, one of only two still in existence in antebellum plantation houses, the others having fallen victim to the torches of Union soldiers, hurricanes, or developers' bulldozers. The magnificent staircase wound upward, to galleries on the second and third floors, crossing over flying bridges, twisting like an M.C. Escher drawing, to a cupola on the roof.

"What I meant to say was that I was surprised the front door was unlocked," Agent Burns said.

"It's always unlocked in the daytime. That's how Daddy wanted it. He said it was inhospitable to lock the door, in case anyone came calling. It's only locked at night, when the servants go home," Aimee told her.

"You mean, you leave it unlocked all day? Anybody can walk in?"

"Yes," Aimee said. "Unless they think it wouldn't be polite; then they ring the bell."

"What happens then?" Burns was astonished that the Trapnells appeared to take no interest in protecting their valuables. Looking around, she saw many objects that could be slipped into a pocket or a backpack and spirited away. On a mahogany console was a jeweled enameled egg, which she suspected was either a genuine Fabergé or an excellent copy. A tall glass case contained antique snuffboxes, ivory miniatures, and an assortment of bibelots. Burns noticed that the case had no lock.

"If they ring the doorbell Lee will answer it. He's our butler now, since Hillman got arrested for murdering my husband and helping to try to destroy the world. If Lee's not around, then one of the maids will do it," Aimee said patiently, as if explaining something to a child.

"But what if a thief came in? There are valuable items here."

"Then Daddy would shoot them," Aimee said. "Daddy always wanted to shoot a burglar. He kept a loaded gun beside him, hoping he'd be burgled, but he never was."

"It was one of the great disappointments of his life," put in Marsh. "Along with *The Ed Sullivan Show* being cancelled."

Burns couldn't believe what she was hearing. "You need a security system."

"What for? Seamus will bark if someone comes in," Aimee said.

Seamus, an elderly Irish setter, snored, fast asleep, in his basket beside the stairs.

Burns decided to let the matter rest for the time being. Noticing a small, bluish-green porcelain dish on the floor, she asked, "Is that your dog's water dish? It's empty."

Marsh picked it up and set it on the table with columns shaped like topless ladies.

"The maids must have put it there when they were dusting. It's not Seamus' dish; his dish is in the kitchen. This is a Northern Song Dynasty brush-washing dish. It was made in China's central Henan province about nine hundred years ago. Note the distinctive duck-egg-blue glaze."

Dooley studied the little dish with interest. "They got some like that at Walmart."

Marsh sniffed disdainfully. "Hardly, unless Walmart bought up the entire run of *Ru* ware made in one particular kiln for only twenty years and is offering it for sale to the public, along with potato chips and those dreadful signs with inane sentiments on them, such as, 'Live, Laugh, Love' or 'This Is My Happy Place.' I can't conceive of why anyone but a moron would display such things. Perhaps they imagine it says something profound about themselves." Marsh's lip curled in distaste. "That dish was appraised as being worth about fifteen million dollars. That's a bit out of reach for the average Walmart shopper."

Marsh had been to a Walmart exactly once, after having been party to the disposal of a body in a swamp. That encounter with discount consumer culture had left him equal parts puzzled and horrified.

"Daddy brought that dish back from China," Aimee told Agent Burns. "He was part of a trade delegation that went there, not long after President Reagan was there. Reagan got China to be friends with America. He invited Daddy personally. He and Daddy used to arm wrestle whenever they got together. Daddy called him Dutch. That was Reagan's nickname."

"I know," said Burns. Her father had met the former B-movie actor on several occasions.

"Affable fellow. Big. Wore cowboy boots. He put considerable faith in astrology. I don't think it's wise to base public policy on the alignment of stars and planets," her father told her.

"Daddy called that dish 'that little old saucer of Li Xiannian's,' That's how he always described it," Aimee said, smiling reminiscently. "Li Xiannian was the president of China back then. Daddy never did understand what was so special about the dish. He said he would have preferred a statue of a dragon, like the one they have in front of the Lucky Fortune, over in Pontahatcha."

Pontahatcha was a nearby town. It was larger than Cobbs and was the home of the Walmart which had made such a negative impression on Marsh. The dragon statue in front of the Lucky Fortune restaurant had scales garishly painted red and gold. It was meant to evoke a sense of the mysterious East to customers hungry for crab Rangoon and pork-fried rice.

"That dragon they got at the Lucky Fortune's made of cement, with rebar holding it down to the blacktop so nobody steals it," said Dooley. "It must weigh purt near a ton. Bringing something that big and heavy over from China wouldn't be easy." He pointed to the blue-green dish. "Better to give your daddy a little old saucer, like this here. Something he could tote home in his valise."

Burns' attention was drawn to an oil painting in a gilt frame of a brown horse. "Isn't that a Stubbs?"

Marsh went and stood beside her, with his hands clasped behind his back. "Brava! Well spotted. You have a good eye for art," he said. "It's by Samuel Spode. Like Stubbs, he was a renowned equine artist. Their work is similar, so much so that art historians sometimes get them confused."

Burns grimaced. "Don't suck up to me, Bad Choices. I hate it when you're being ingratiating."

Aimee spoke up. "Spode and Stubbs are probably the best-known of the equine artists, along with Théodore Géricault. Of course, there's also Degas, although his work is more often associated with the ballet."

It was as if Seamus the Irish setter had spoken, so surprising was it to hear Aimee hold forth knowledgeably on a topic other than snakes, or fashion design. She looked around at their shocked faces. "What? Daddy was an art collector. I learned a lot from listening to him."

She nodded at the painting of the horse. "Daddy's mama, Grandma Norma, brought that picture back from England. Her sister married the Duke of Balmoral, a man by the name of St. Simon. He had a big old house that was bursting at the seams with old paintings. He was almost flat broke when he met Great-aunt Maggie. He was so relieved to marry an American heiress that he was happy to give some of his paintings to Grandma Norma. Besides the Spode, he gave her a Landseer and a Gainsborough. They're upstairs. Daddy didn't care for them; he preferred modern art."

"If you like art, we've got some Picassos," Benjamin told Burns. "There's one here. The others are on loan to museums."

Burns made a mental note to bring up the topic of having a security system installed as soon as possible. *Cameras,* she thought. *Motion sensors. Keypads. Alarms.*

Her mental list-making was interrupted by Jubilee appearing at the top of the stairs leading to the second-floor gallery. Upon sight of her cousin, she squealed, "Benjamin!"

Seamus raised his head and took in the newcomers. His tail thumped in greeting. Then he yawned, stretched, and curled up in his basket again.

"Hi, Jubilee. What's up?" Benjamin said.

Jubilee adored her older cousin. Ignoring the others, she bounded down the stairs and grabbed him by the hand. "I got a turtle. Daddy caught it in the swamp out back. I'll show you. Are you staying overnight? If you sleep in the room next to mine, we can tap on the wall to each other, like we did last time."

"That'll be fun," Benjamin said, tickled by her enthusiasm.

"Where are your mommy and daddy?" Aimee asked the child.

"Out back, showing Aunt Yamma the greenhouses," she said.

There were three large, domed conservatories behind the house, put there by Norma Trapnell, the lady who had been given a Stubbs, a Gainsborough, and a Landseer by her English brother-in-law. The conservatories were surrounded by sixty-eight acres of meticulously maintained gardens. There was a boxwood maze, an observation tower, an Elizabethan-style knot garden, fountains, and the garden's centerpiece: a water feature consisting of a series of limestone steps over which water from the swamp endlessly circulated, powered by underground pumps. Norma had designed it all herself, despite having had no formal training in landscape architecture.

Her artistic streak was said to have been passed down to her granddaughter, Aimee. Marsh sometimes remarked on it, quoting Arthur Conan Doyle's great detective. "Art in the blood," he'd say, looking pointedly at Aimee. "It's liable to take the strangest forms."

"Let's bring everyone inside," Burns said.

Aimee chose that moment to instruct her niece in etiquette.

"Jubilee, we have a guest," she said, placing her hand on Burns' arm and drawing the FBI agent forward. "What do we say when we have a guest?"

"I dunno," Jubilee muttered, scuffling her feet, and looking at the floor.

"Yes, you do. You go, 'How do you do? My name is Jubilee Trapnell. I am pleased to make your acquaintance.' That's what you should say," Aimee told her.

The child giggled, "You sound funny when you talk like that. You sound like a cartoon cat."

Aimee forced herself to smile pleasantly, while mentally resolving to give Jubilee something she wouldn't like for her birthday, underwear, perhaps, or a toothbrush.

Burns bent down so she was at eye level with Jubilee. "My name's Carson Burns. I'm pleased to make your acquaintance. This is such a pretty house, full of pretty things." She pointed to the Spode painting, adding, "like that pretty picture of a horse."

"I can paint a better horse than that," Jubilee scoffed. "Its head is too little. Horses' heads are bigger than that. I have a pony, so I know what horses look like."

"I bet you take real good care of that pony," Dooley Voight said. He was not averse to fawning in order to ingratiate himself with the Trapnells. It didn't matter that Jubilee was only seven years old. If he made a good impression on her now, it would improve the chances of her hiring him to handle any legal issues she might have when she was older.

"I can paint anything," Jubilee boasted. "This one time, I painted a picture of a dog, just like one Poblano Peahassle painted. Daddy said nobody could tell the difference, my picture was so good. Daddy was going to sell it for a lot of money, pretending Poblano Peahassle painted it, but then he didn't have to, because..."

"That's enough, Jubilee," Marsh cut in nervously. "Ms. Burns isn't interested in our little family activities."

Agent Burns thought she might be very interested in what sounded like an attempt to commit art fraud. She reminded herself that she was there to protect the Trapnells, not to gather evidence against them.

"Jubilee is a lovely name," she told the child.

Jubilee scowled. "Hailey Branwell called me cherries jubilee. I told her to shut her fat face or I'd shut it for her."

"Ladies don't tell each other to shut their fat faces," Aimee said.

"Hailey Branwell is one of her little friends from school," she explained to Burns.

"She'd not my friend, and if she keeps calling me names, I'm going to make her sorry she was ever born," Jubilee said darkly.

"Ms. Burns works for the FBI. It's like being a police officer, only more important," Aimee told her.

"Okay," Jubilee said, anxious to get away. "I'm pleased to make your acquaintance, Ms. Burns. I'm going now. Bye."

She headed toward the stairs, towing a bemused Benjamin behind her.

"Hold it!" Aimee ordered, in a voice that could have frozen boiling water. "We have another guest, Mister Voight. You didn't greet him."

"He was here earlier; I said hello to him then," the child protested.

"You should have acknowledged him when you saw him this time, and me and your Uncle Marsh. You should have greeted all of us, not just Benjamin."

"Sorry. Hi, y'all," Jubilee said.

"Think nothing of it, darlin'. You go on upstairs and show your cousin that turtle," Dooley told her.

Jubilee quickly complied, before Aimee could chastise her further.

Dooley chuckled, "She's got spirit. I like a child with spirit."

"She's got too much spirit, in my opinion," Aimee replied.

"There ain't no such thing as too much spirit," the lawyer said. "All my clients got plenty of spirit."

Clients like that crook, Peach Walker, Aimee thought sourly. Out loud, she said, "Let's go in the Gentlemen's Parlor. Marsh, you go get Trainor and Palmer and Yamma."

"Care to join me?" Marsh asked Agent Burns. "There are some interesting plants out back."

Burns had a suspicion about what sort of plants they were. "If you've got opium poppies and hallucinogenic mushrooms growing out there, I'm warning you right now that you'd better get rid of them."

Marsh raised his eyebrows in mock surprise. "Good gracious! There's nothing like that. You have a lurid imagination, Agent Burns. Do they encourage trainees at Quantico to envision sinister possibilities lurking at every turn? It must make even the most mundane activities seem fraught with peril."

Burns didn't reply. She was thinking about what sort of vegetation might be growing on the premises. Wasn't there a tree so toxic that it could kill someone, just by standing close to it? She thought there was. If anyone was likely to nurture a deadly tree, it would be the Trapnells.

Marsh laughed. "Relax. There's nothing illegal out there. I'll give you the grand tour later. Go in and have a seat. I'll go find the others."

CHAPTER SEVEN
MONEY FOR NOTHING

The adult Trapnells were gathered in the ground-floor room known as the Gentlemen's Parlor, along with Agent Burns and Yamma. Dooley had gone home, anticipating how much he would bill the family for his day's work on their behalf. He ran the figures over and over in his head, feeling like he had won the lottery. He slapped the steering wheel of the Lexus and laughed in delight.

"Hot dog! I can afford a new bass boat!"

The Gentlemen's Parlor was the twin of a room in the opposite wing, designated as the Ladies Parlor when the house was built in 1831. Like those of the Ladies Parlor, the walls of the Gentlemen's Parlor were originally decorated with hand-painted wallpaper, brought back from China aboard the brigantine *Hetty Gwinn*. The ship was owned by an ancestor of the current crop of Trapnells. It was sunk off Port Royal, South Carolina, while attempting to evade the Union blockade during the Civil War.

The Trapnells belonged to a segment of society which proudly identified itself as "fine old Southern families." The Trapnell family history in Georgia wasn't all that old. The first of their ancestors to set foot on North American soil was a remittance man. He was a thorough reprobate and unrepentant scoundrel whose father sent him over from Scotland in 1800 with an annual allowance and a stern warning to never return. There wasn't anything fine about him, or his descendants. That didn't matter. What mattered was that the Trapnells considered themselves gentry, even Trainor, who had no more social graces than an earthworm.

Like others of their ilk, The Trapnells could recite every detail of their genealogy. What they didn't know they made up. They could hold forth on the voyages of the *Hetty Gwinn,* and of the sad fate of its final, blockade-running captain. He died, not in action, a martyr to the Lost Cause, as his descendants liked to pretend, but from a venereal disease he picked up in a Savannah whorehouse. He was invariably described as "dashing" and "gallant." The father of the Trapnell siblings, canny, unscrupulous Blanton Trapnell, was named after him.

When Blanton began to amass his fortune in the nineteen fifties, he left the Ladies Parlor untouched, with its carved rosewood furnishings upholstered in faded red velveteen, and its wallpaper depicting an exotic landscape with half-moon bridges and curve-roofed temples and ladies in kimonos. Blanton thought the Ladies Parlor was best left undisturbed as a place for the ladies to retreat when the men started talking about business or politics. The ladies cared every bit as much about business and politics as the men did; they only pretended they didn't in order to make the men feel smart and capable. That way, everyone was happy.

Having abandoned the Ladies Parlor to the women of the household, Blanton took charge of redecorating the Gentlemen's Parlor. He stripped the priceless hand-painted paper from the walls and had the furnishings carted to the dump. He replaced the graceful French antiques, some of which had been made expressly for Marie Antoinette, with austere midcentury modern pieces, all black leather and chrome and smoked glass. The result pleased him. It had a businesslike quality, like that of the furnishings of the executive offices of the headquarters of IBM or Kodak. Blanton loved business, not just the accumulation of money, but its fierce, adversarial nature.

Blanton was a throwback to the robber barons of the nineteenth century, ruthless men, hard as coffin nails, who built railroads and drilled for oil, not caring how many lives were wrecked in the process. Blanton relished clashing with his competitors, outbidding them, underselling them, and eventually driving them to their knees in defeat and humiliation. He was by no means a nice man, but there was no doubt that he was a successful one.

Agent Burns saw Benjamin hadn't been wrong about the Picasso. There it was, in the artist's unmistakable style, its bold brush strokes depicting a black dog sitting on its haunches. Both its eyes were on the same side of its head, which was tilted enquiringly as it studied a bird with long, spindly legs.

The walls of the Gentlemen's Parlor were painted stark white, and were thickly hung with works by a bevy of renowned twentieth-century artists, among them Lichtenstein, Pollock, Mondrian, Matisse, and Warhol. Long windows opened onto a broad expanse of lawn, perfect as a putting green.

Atop a black marble column was a polished chrome sculpture of a rabbit, its puffy contours resembling a balloon animal. *That's a Koons,* Burns, thought, amazed. A huge bronze sculpture which looked like a lopsided bagel took up one corner of the room. *Good God, they've got a Henry Moore, too*, Barnes thought. She'd never seen such a collection outside of a museum, and this was just a tiny portion of what the Trapnells owned. She couldn't even imagine how much the art in this room was worth.

Lee, the butler, was out running errands. Two maids, Janelle and Anea, brought in refreshments. There were egg salad and watercress sandwiches, and for Trainor, his favorite: peanut butter and jelly. On a tray were ice-filled glasses and a cut-glass pitcher of sweet tea. The maids hung around, mesmerized by Agent Burns, having never met an FBI agent before.

"What does a person have to do to get in the FBI?" Janelle asked.

Burns explained the requirements.

"I'm twenty-three. That's old enough," Janelle said excitedly. "And I got a driver's license, and I'm a U.S., citizen, born right here, in Boyce County. I qualify!"

"But the college, you ain't got that," Anea pointed out.

"Uh-uh. You wrong. I got a cosmetology degree from Pontahatcha Junior College. So there," Janelle told her, and stuck out her tongue.

Refusing to be quailed, Anea asked Burns, "How much money you make?"

Burns looked around at the Trapnells, hoping one of them would gently remonstrate the young woman for asking such a rude question. To her surprise, no one said a word. Instead, they leaned closer, curious to hear the answer.

"I made a little over a hundred thousand dollars last year," she said.

Janelle clapped her hands. "Whoo-ee! That's it! I'm signing up!"

"You got to be able to run fast, and climb ropes. I seen it in a movie. It's like the Army," Anea told her.

"You're better off stayin' where you're at," Trainor advised Janelle. "Alls you got to do around here is a little dustin' and vacuumin' and helpin' Louetta out sometimes."

Louetta Waites was their cook. She had a profitable sideline going in the form of a catering business, which she ran out of the kitchen at White Oaks, with the blessing of the Trapnell siblings. The Trapnells didn't spend much time at White Oaks. They were usually occupied elsewhere, designing clothing, or selling weapons, or, in Trainor's case, just taking it easy.

Trainor had only a foggy understanding of what working for a living entailed, but it didn't prevent him from lecturing Janelle on the subject of employment. "Half the time nobody's here except for you and Anea and Louetta and Lee. You got the run of the place. You spend all day gabbin' and watchin' TV while gettin' paid to do it. I wouldn't mind gettin' paid to do nothin' all day."

Nobody pointed out that it was exactly how he'd always lived, in luxurious idleness, thanks to his father's generosity.

"I thought about joining the Army," Palmer mused, daintily patting her lips with a starched linen napkin. She was a tiny, stylish woman in a Lily Pulitzer sundress and Balenciaga sandals. In contrast, her husband had on cut-off jeans shorts and a t-shirt advertising a business called Caligula's Roman-Style Buffet and Titty Bar.

A smile of satisfaction spread across Palmer's face as she examined the diamond and platinum eternity ring on the third finger of her right hand. It was a gift from Trainor, a conciliatory offering after one of their quarrels. Its three diamonds were larger than the ones in her friend Chandler Woodbury's eternity ring. Thinking about how angry that had made Chandler pleased Palmer. She was resentful about Chandler's acceptance into the Daughters of Arsinoe, a venerable Atlanta women's organization. Palmer's application was still pending. Would Chandler do something to prevent Palmer from becoming a member? Palmer feared she might. She would do the same to Candler, if their situations were reversed.

Until Chandler had gotten in, Palmer hadn't cared one whit about the Daughters of Arsinoe, thinking them a bunch of boring old ladies. She had been satisfied with belonging to Druid Hills Golf Club, and the Buckhead Ladies Luncheon Society, and the Book Belles. The latter was a book club which met on Wednesday afternoons in members' homes.

Palmer wasn't much of a reader. Her taste in literature ran to the type of unlikely historical fiction in which the captain of a pirate ship romances a woman who sells flowers in a stall at London's Covent Garden Market, with the pirate later revealing himself to be the king of Sweden. She dealt with meetings of the Book Belles by trying to get the gist of whichever book was being discussed by studying the cover for clues.

Palmer had created a club of her own. It was called Pony Mommies. She had started it to support Jubilee, who owned a pony to whom she was feverishly devoted. Pony Mommies was made up of Palmer and three other women whose children owned ponies. As clubs went, it wasn't up to much, but Palmer wasn't deterred. She'd had windbreakers made with the club's name on them and was hoping Pony Mommies would become the next big thing to hit the Atlanta social scene.

Based on the belief that it was never too early to launch a child into society, she had enrolled Jubilee in Little Lads and Lassies, a club for boys and girls, aged five to ten. Its aim was to foster skills in ballroom dancing, and eating neatly, without spilling, while making polite conversation. So far, Jubilee was doing well, despite Trainor's advice that the best way to eat anything was to grab the biggest piece and consume it hurriedly, using one's fingers.

Palmer had pleaded with her husband to have better table manners, but to no avail.

"You eat like you were raised by wolves," she complained.

"I wish," he replied. "That would be awesome."

Ever since Chandler became a Daughter of Arsinoe, Palmer had lost interest in all her other clubs. All she could think about was getting into the Daughters of Arsinoe, so Chandler would quit boasting about it.

Continuing with her thoughts on enlisting in the Army, Palmer said, "The uniforms are cute, and they let you wear makeup, as long as you don't wear too much. They even let you wear earrings, not hoops, just posts—pearls and such—but still, those Army girls look cute. And they train you for a career when you get out." She looked around at the others, to see if they were impressed by the Army's largesse. "I almost signed up, but I found out the Army makes you get up early. I don't like getting up early, so I married Trainor instead. It turned out good, didn't it, Boo Bear?"

She smiled at Trainor, and patted his hairy thigh. Having eaten three peanut butter sandwiches, Trainor was idly shelling boiled peanuts, popping them in his mouth and dropping the shells on the antique silk Kashan carpet.

"It sure did, Chicken Legs," he told Palmer through a mouthful of peanuts.

Just then, an anguished cry came from somewhere above them. It sounded like the plaintive wail of a ghost, or perhaps a banshee. It echoed through the galleries, and was funneled down the double-reverse staircase, through the entry hall and into the Gentlemen's Parlor.

"Sheldon! Don't!"

Burns sprang to her feet, her hand instinctively reaching for the Glock 9mm sidearm she wore in an underarm holster. "What was that?"

Trainor shelled another peanut. "Just Jubilee. She's loud for a little bitty thing, ain't she?" He seemed proud that his child was able to produce such a bloodcurdling scream. "Her turtle must've bit her. It's called Sheldon."

Palmer selected a watercress sandwich from the plate on the kidney-shaped coffee table. "I thought of that name. Clever, isn't it? A turtle called Sheldon? It's got a shell. That's why it's called Sheldon."

"You sure are smart, Chicken Legs," Trainor said admiringly.

"What kind of turtle is it?" Aimee asked.

"Snapper," Trainor said, chewing on a peanut.

Marsh reached for an egg salad sandwich. "There you go, then. Snapping turtles bite, hence the name. Jubilee learned a valuable lesson."

He took a bite of sandwich and nodded his head appreciatively. "I love Louetta's egg salad. I know for a fact that she puts ground mustard in it, and I can detect something else, possibly tarragon. She refuses to disclose the recipe, no matter how I beg."

Burns was shocked they were being so cavalier about Jubilee's distress. "It could have taken her finger off."

"Don't sound like it," Janelle said, listening to the loud sobs coming from upstairs. "It probably just gave her a good nip. My brother Darnell, got his little finger bit off by a snapper." She held up her finger and pointed to where her brother's injury took place. "It only bit it partway off; a doctor cut off the rest. He had to, since it was hangin' by a sliver of skin. It wouldn't have been no good to him like that."

Burns was puzzled. Her acquaintance with Marsh had prepared her for his family being unconventional, but they were even more unusual than she had expected. This beautifully maintained plantation house, this room where they sat, full of priceless works of art, the front door left unlocked, the casual way the servants interacted with their employers. It baffled her. These people were very, very strange.

"Benjamin is with her. If she got her finger bit off, he'd come down and tell us," Aimee said. "I'm sure he has everything under control."

"Unless the turtle got him, too," Janelle said.

"That's right," Anea agreed. "It could have got them both. They could be up there right now, bleeding to death."

Trainor laughed. "You girls is crazy. It's a turtle, not a man-eating tiger. Turtles ain't never killed nobody."

"All this talk of killing makes me think of those poor young men," said Yamma.

Trainor asked, "Who you talkin' about, Aunt Yamma? You talkin' about those guys you buried? Is that what's botherin' you?"

Yamma wrung her hands. "Yes, poor things!"

"Don't get yourself worked up over the likes of them," Trainor told her severely, shelling another peanut. "People that get shot in the head in a field, out in the middle of nowhere, ain't the kind of people worth gettin' worked up over. You shouldn't have buried 'em. That's too much work for a lady your age. Diggin' graves is time-consumin'. How long did it take you, anyway?"

"Several hours for each one. I don't know exactly. I didn't think to time it," Yamma said apologetically.

"Say four hours each? That ain't bad. And they wasn't shallow graves, was they? You buried 'em deep."

"Any job worth doing is worth doing well," she said.

Trainor considered her, a look of pride on his bearded face. "If that don't beat all! That must be some kind of record for a lady your age."

Yamma smiled modestly. "I wouldn't know about that."

"It's not polite to tell a lady that she's old," Palmer told her husband. Addressing Yamma, she said, "Trainor's right; it could have been some kind of record. You ought to get in touch with the company that puts out the book of world records, see if you qualify to get written up in it."

Yamma demurred. "I wouldn't want to put them to any trouble."

"What I don't get is how come you buried them?" Anea asked. "Why didn't you just leave them where you found them?"

"Yeah, leave them for birds to eat. That's called a sky burial. I watched a video online about it," Janelle said, sounding deliciously thrilled. "They do it in foreign places. It's part of their religion. It's sick, the way vultures eat the guts and the eyeballs."

They all considered that for a moment, picturing it. Then Janelle added, "You know what else is sick? The body farm the FBI got. They got dead people lying right out in the open, rotting."

"My goodness!" said Yamma.

"Dang!" said Trainor, and reached for another peanut.

"You ever been there?" Janelle asked Agent Burns.

Burns had, but she didn't want to go into it. When the others stared at her, their eyes begging her for details, she sighed and relented. "It's called the Forensic Anthropology Center. It's in Knoxville. People request that their bodies be donated there after they pass away."

"Ooh! Gross," Janelle said. "And you were there? You saw the dead bodies? Were they naked?"

"I attended a course there on outdoor crime scene investigation," Burns said, choosing her words carefully, refusing to give in to Janelle's desire for gruesome details. "They do important work. It's all done very respectfully."

Aimee grimaced in distaste. "It doesn't sound very respectful to me. When I die, I'm getting a big mausoleum. I'm considering one with a Babylonian motif, with a frieze of elephants and palm fronds going around the top. Classical, you know?"

"We already got a mausoleum out back," Trainor reminded her.

"My husband was murdered in it. I would prefer not to be entombed there, thank you very much. It would bring back bad memories for me," Aimee said frostily.

"Getting back to the dead men, who were they?" Marsh asked Burns.

Addressing the two maids, the FBI agent said, "I'd like to talk to you and Ms. Louetta separately, along with everyone else who works here. That includes the butler, Lee, isn't that his name? And the groundskeepers and gardeners and everyone else employed on the property. Let's say tomorrow morning, at ten."

"You could meet on the patio behind the kitchen. There's plenty of seating for everyone. It's pleasant out there that time of day," Marsh suggested.

"They want us to leave now, so they can talk privately among themselves," Anea told Janelle. The two young women stood up and shook out their hair. They adjusted their shorts and smoothed down their t-shirts. Janelle's had the logo of a band called Seven Layers of Ants on it. Anea's bore the ominous warning DON'T PLAY THE FOOL WITH ME.

Burns, who thought maids were supposed to wear uniforms, put it down as another eccentricity of this odd household.

CHAPTER EIGHT
THE ASSASSINS

"Who was they? Those guys Aunt Yamma buried?" Trainor asked Burns when Anea and Janelle had left the room.

"One of them is believed to have been Ulakistani. According to my contact in the State Department, he was traveling on a Russian passport," Burns said.

Marsh frowned. "But the Ulakistanis hate the Russians. The feeling is mutual. There's a Russian saying that goes, 'Better to marry a pig than to speak to an Ulakistani.' The Ulakistanis have a similar one about Russians, but it's so rude that I won't repeat it."

"How did he get a Russian passport?" Aimee asked.

"Good question," said Burns. "The State Department is looking into it. Moscow claims to know nothing about it."

Marsh selected a peanut from the paper bag on the kidney-shaped table. He shelled it and deposited the shell neatly in a chrome dish. "That's typical. Moscow always insists it knows nothing when incidents occur which might prove embarrassing for them."

"Who was the other man?" Yamma asked. "They were both young, and rather good-looking, I thought, although it was hard to tell, what with them having big holes in their heads. I suppose that was a result of being shot. I would never own a gun. I'm afraid of them. Guns are dangerous. No offense, Marsh. I know that's how you make your living, selling guns and whatnot."

"No offense taken, Aunt Yamma. Guns *are* dangerous; that's why people want them," Marsh told her serenely.

"The other man was American. His name was Robert Joseph Gaffney, alias Bobby Joe Cullum, alias Mark "Melee" Monaghan. He had an extensive criminal record. He was what's called a honky-tonk hitman, a bottom-feeder, someone willing to do just about anything for money," Burns said.

"People like that are disgusting," Trainor said indignantly, ignoring the fact that his best friend, Peach Walker, was very much like the late Robert Joseph Gaffney in his willingness to engage in criminal activity for financial gain.

"I know an Angeline Gaffney from the Capitol City Club, back home in Atlanta. Maybe they're kin. Where was he from?" Palmer asked Burns.

"Vero Beach, Florida," Burns said.

"I don't believe I've ever been there. Is it nice?"

"I didn't think so," Trainor said. "I was there one time. I went in a store to get a cold drink and when I come out, what do I see? Some damn fool had run into my car, that's what I seen. Put a big dent in the side and drove off without a care in the world. Course they didn't leave no note. People who run into your car never leave a note."

Turning to Yamma, he said, "You shouldn't oughta have buried them, not at your age. It's too strenuous for a lady your age. Next time you find dead bodies, call the police. Let them deal with it, you hear?"

"All right, Trainor," Yamma said meekly. "I didn't mean to cause a fuss. If I come across any more dead bodies, I promise I'll call the police."

"Who shot them? Do the police have any leads?" Palmer asked Agent Burns.

"The investigation is ongoing," Burns said.

"Who cares?" Trainor said, munching on a peanut. "They was bad guys and now they're dead. Good riddance."

CHAPTER NINE
PARDON THE INTERRUPTION

The guest room where Agent Burns was staying had an antique four-poster bed, with carved, barley-twist bedposts. It had been installed in that room shortly after the house was built, having come up the Mississippi from New Orleans on a keelboat. The bed had chintz curtains which could be pulled closed, creating a snug hideaway. Burns, who had spent many happy hours building blanket forts when she was a child, pulled the curtains closed and climbed in. It was better than a blanket fort. The mattress was perfect, neither too firm nor too soft. The sheets were likewise perfect: simultaneously crisp and luxuriously soft.

The guest room was nicer than any of the rooms in her apartment in Atlanta. The wool rug was thick, its pastel colors perfectly complementing the curtains around the bed and on the French window leading to a private balcony. Not matching, but complementing. *That's how expensive décor works*, Burns thought. Anyone can buy a rug and matching curtains. It took serious coin to create a room like this.

There was a painting on one wall of a Newfoundland dog. It stood on a rocky shoreline, looking out to sea, beside a rowboat draped with fishing nets. The dog looked glum, as if it understood that its owner had drowned. Burns thought the painting was the one by Edwin Landseer, which Aimee had referred to earlier. *The Gainsborough must be up here somewhere,* she thought.

It had been a long day. Burns changed into her pajamas and unpacked her bag. She put her clothes away, neatly hanging her suits–two black and one dark blue–in the wardrobe, an antique, like the bed. She was reading emails on her laptop when a quick *rat-a-tat* came at the door, followed by a man poking his head in.

At the sight of her, the man froze. "Pardon the interruption," he said softly. He withdrew his head and closed the door.

That must be Lee, the butler, thought Burns. She locked the door, then went back to reading her emails.

Meanwhile, the Madman of the Steppes, aka Andrej Yakov Temirkhan Asgarov Sadyharbaghi aka Andy Jacobs resumed his tiptoed progress along the second-floor corridor, in search of Marsh. He thought he had found Marsh's room, but it contained a beautiful lady in pajamas.

If one imagined the Ulakistani tyrant to be a diabolical-looking giant of a man, a cross between Peter the Great and Rasputin, they would be disappointed. The individual currently styling himself as Andy Jacobs was five feet, nine inches tall, with narrow shoulders and a little paunch. He had thinning reddish-brown hair and was deceptively mild in appearance. One might take him for an insurance salesman.

"This dacha is not bad, but it is nothing compared to the splendor of the Presidential Palace," he muttered to himself. "I shall return to the Presidential Palace when I regain my rightful place as beloved head of state of the glorious nation which is Eastern Europe's greatest source of manganese ore. And when I do, boy oh boy, are people going to get it for staging a coup against my benevolent regime."

He tried to recall which of the identical ivory-colored doors belonged to the room of his friend, Marshov Trapnellovich. Wouldn't he be surprised when he saw his old friend Andy!

Earlier, the butler, a fellow named Lee, had shown him where Marsh's room was. Lee and the Madman of the Steppes had hit it off, bonding over their mutual hatred of Kim Jong-un, Supreme Leader of North Korea. Lee's grandparents had escaped from there, having to leave behind everything they owned. They passed on their bitterness to their children and their grandchildren, none of whom had ever set foot in North Korea.

"When I return to Ulakistan, perhaps I will send that stuck-up little *varenyky* a present, one which will blow up all of Pyongyang," Andy muttered. "We'll see what he thinks about *that!*"

Ulakistan did not possess nuclear weapons. Andy intended to remedy that as soon as he was able.

Why did Andy hate Kim Jong-un? The answer was simple. He hated him because the North Korean dictator had never acknowledged him in any way, either to praise Ulakistan (and by extension Andy) or to belittle it. It was as if he didn't know or care that Ulakistan existed. It was an insult that was not to be tolerated. Andy planned to demonstrate to Kim Jong-un that Ulakistan did, indeed, exist, by bombing the daylights out of North Korea. The thought made him smile.

Aha! Here was the room of Marshov Trapnellovich! Andy recognized it by the painting hanging on the wall opposite the door. It was the Gainsborough that Agent Burns had wondered about. It depicted a man in a tricorne hat and knee-breeches standing beneath a tree. Sheep grazed in the background. To be honest, it was not one of Gainsborough's best.

Andy threw open the door.

"Your eyes do not deceive you," he announced to a startled Marsh. "For it is indeed I, your bosom companion, Andrej Yakov Temirkhan Asgarov Sadyharbaghi, whom you know as Andy Jacobs! Surprise!"

Then he noticed Marsh had company.

"Pardon me, I did not realize you were in bed with a lady. I will return at another time," he said, and started to close the door.

"Don't be ridiculous. This isn't a lady; it's my sister. Come in. What are you doing here? I thought you were in Texas," Marsh asked.

"We're not in bed together," Aimee put in. "I'm sitting on the bed, talking to Marsh. We're both fully clothed."

"Of course. Far be it from me to imply that anything indelicate was going on," Andy said, smiling roguishly at her. To Marsh he said, "If I had such a beautiful sister I would buy her nice clothes, not *schmulke,* like what she has on, all ragged, with holes."

Aimee was flattered that Andy found her beautiful, but was insulted by his opinion of her outfit. "I designed these clothes myself. People pay a lot of money for the clothes I design. And for your information, it's normal in America for a woman to sit on her brother's bed, talking to him while he's lying down," she said sternly.

"Of that I have no doubt, beautiful lady. I have watched your reality television. *Ebozhe miy!* Such goings-on! I do not judge, however. There is another lady in a room down the corridor, a beautiful dark lady. I am impressed. Marshov Trapnellovich has not one but two beautiful ladies in his house."

"It's perfectly innocent," Marsh said. "That other lady is with the FBI."

"Naturally," Andy said soothingly. "Your secret police, yes?" He turned to Aimee. "I am here to lend assistance to your brother in his hour of need."

"I don't need assistance," Marsh told him.

"Ah, but you do." Andy seated himself in the chair at the rolltop desk. He swiveled it around, giving Marsh a knowing smile.

"What kind of assistance? And how did you get away from the ranch? I thought the Secret Service was watching you?"

Andy's shoulders shook with laughter. "The Secret Service? My friend, the ones they had guarding me could not guard a plate of *nalésniki* from a child!"

Marsh suspected Andy was right. From what he knew about federal agents, some of them were like Burns, in that they took their duties seriously. Others only did the bare minimum.

"How did you get here?" he asked Andy.

Andy puffed himself up proudly. "I was clever. I am not called the Sly Fox of the Frozen Tundra for nothing."

"I thought you were the Madman of the Steppes," Aimee said.

"I am both, beautiful lady. I got away by lulling my captors into complaisance. I pretended to have no interest in escaping. After a while, they let me ride in the truck when they went into town to get the, what do you call them? The groceries. I sat nicely in the truck two, three, four, five times, until they thought it would be all right for them to leave me there while they went into a place that sells your terrible overpriced American coffee. That is when I got out and ran to the highway, swift as an arrow in flight. I stuck out my thumb and got a ride with a man who told me all about something he called a paleolithic diet." He pronounced it, "pal-leo-leethic."

Andy went on, "This man, he drove me for hours, talking of his caveman diet. Then I got another ride, and another, and another, until finally, I am here before you now."

"Won't they be able to find you?" Aimee asked.

"You mean by using the little tracking devices they sewed in the linings of my trousers? The little plastic buttons containing the, what is it called? The GPS?" Andy laughed scornfully. "What fools they are! The little devices they thought they were so clever by concealing in my shoes? Bah! I found those within one day of my arrival at the ranch. The mobile phone they gave me I threw in a ditch. I told the first man who gave me a ride that I was making a pilgrimage to Memphis, to visit the home of Elvis Presley, king of the rock and roll! I told the other people who stopped for me different stories. They can look for me at the home of Elvis, or in Philadelphia, where there is the Liberty Bell, or in Boston, home of the baked beans, or in any of the other places where I said I was going. They will not find me. I am like the Scarlet Pimpernel, able to vanish without a trace from the clutches of my captors!"

He looked at Aimee to see if she was impressed. She didn't appear to be. That only served to deepen his admiration for her. He rolled his chair closer and whispered, "Now I will tell you something, beautiful lady. I am here with my friend Marshov Trapnellovich, to save him from terrible danger."

"What kind of danger?" Marsh asked.

"Terrible danger," Andy repeated.

Aimee yawned. This was getting boring. First, nutty old Yamma turned up at White Oaks and now this egotistical former dictator. "Marsh is always in danger. He likes it that way, otherwise he'd have a normal profession, or no profession at all, like my other brother."

"This is different," their uninvited guest said.

"What's different about it?" Marsh asked.

"This time it is the Illuminati."

Marsh laughed. "Oh, come on! You're joking. There is no such thing. There was once, but not anymore. It was a secret society, formed during the Enlightenment. It started in Bavaria, as I recall. It opposed religious influence over public life and abuses of state power. The Bavarian government outlawed it, encouraged by the Catholic Church. That was around the end of the eighteenth century. It no longer exists. Only nuts believe in it, conspiracy theorists, the tinfoil hat brigade, people who claim Earth is hollow, or flat, or that the moon landing was faked. They think the Illuminati is made up of members the social elite, who have cooked up a nefarious plot to rule the world. It's ridiculous. And why would they be after me? It doesn't make sense. Come one, Andy, be serious."

"I am serious. Think about it; what better way to hide the existence of a threat than to pretend it is not real? As the decadent French poet Baudelaire said of Satan, 'The best trick of the Devil was in convincing the world he did not exist.' That is what the Illuminati have done, my friend, by making it seem as if they are only a fantasy, one believed in by cracked plates."

"Crackpots, you mean," Aimee said.

Andy nodded. "Crazy people, yes, but the people who are saying this are not crazy. The Secret Service people said it at the ranch in Texas. They spoke of a famous woman who is saying it, on the Twitter and the Instagram."

"Which famous woman?" Aimee asked.

"The famous woman known as Baby Patty Cake. She said it, on the Twitter and on the Instagram, to her many followers, not once but several times."

Marsh sat up higher in bed. "I never heard of her. Are you sure she mentioned me by name?"

"She spoke the name of your family. Of that I am certain."

"Oh, for Pete's sake," said Aimee, thoroughly disgusted. "I thought you were going to say it was someone with some credibility. Baby Patty Cake is just making it up to get attention. She's horrible. She threatened me in an elevator one time. If she talked about our family, it's because she's mad because I refused to give her some clothes for free. She's a bully. I wouldn't believe a word she says."

Andy didn't appear convinced. "Listen," said Aimee. "There is no Illuminati. Who do you believe, me and Marsh, or a woman who threatens people in elevators?"

"Beautiful sister of Marshov Trapnellovitch..." Andy began, but Aimee cut him off.

"I'm not just Marsh's sister," she told him angrily. "I'm an internationally known fashion designer. During Fashion Week in Paris, I'm always seated in the front row, *always,* do you hear?"

Andy nodded dumbly as Aimee continued, "I was married to a count, and then to a margrave. I am Aimee Louise Trapnell d'Olficcio de Monteleone von Helgern, I have a lot of money. I am a very successful person."

She glared at him, as if defying him to say otherwise.

Andy regarded her worshipfully. "Such fire! Such beauty! It is as if a terrifying wild animal is before me!" He kissed his fingertips. "Dear lady, you are marvelous."

Aimee simpered. "Thanks."

"Dear lady, is it possible that one so beautiful and filled with fire could, by some miracle, be single?"

"It is, and I am," Aimee said.

"Ah," Andy breathed, scooting his chair closer to where she lounged on the bed. "I am currently without a wife, the last four having met with tragic accidents that were not of my making, despite what my enemies said. At some point, when I resume control of my country, might you consider becoming the beloved first lady of the glorious nation of Ulakistan?"

He raised an inquiring eyebrow. Aimee didn't appear surprised by the offer. She assumed any man would want to marry her.

Andy sweetened the deal. "Your portrait would be on all the currency. There would be statues of you everywhere. The people would love you, the way the people of Argentina loved the lady from the movie starring Madonna."

"Evita? Really? I could be like Evita and wave to my adoring fans from a balcony? And they would chant my name? That's an interesting offer. I'll think about it." The idea of being the wife of a head of state, one who would be in power for life, since Ulakistan was a democracy in name only, appealed to her.

"Please do," Andy said.

"Can we get back to the problem at hand?" Marsh asked.

"The Illuminati?" Andy asked.

"They're not real. There aren't any secret societies anymore," Aimee said.

"Actually, there are," Marsh said.

"Okay, I suppose there are, technically speaking. There was the one that cost us the best butler we ever had," Aimee said, hastily adding, "and killed my husband," when Marsh raised an ironic eyebrow.

Aimee's love for her late second husband, Franz-Albert, had cooled by the time of his death. While she no longer much cared for him, she savored the respectful reaction that resulted whenever she mentioned, oh so casually, that he was a margrave. The best tables at restaurants, entrée to exclusive events, white-glove service, all appeared as if by magic once the word was dropped. Americans are awed by hereditary titles, even ones they don't understand. Aimee had come to realize that being the widow of a margrave wasn't as good as being married to a live one.

Annoyed, she went on, "That secret society wasn't trying to control the world, the way people say the Illuminati do; they were trying to destroy it. And Freemasons are real. Long ago, people thought they ran everything, but they've gotten tame nowadays. Daddy was one. They make their members swear an oath, on pain of death, not to tell outsiders anything about what they do. If they tell, they get strangled and their guts are ripped out. Daddy told me all about it. He taught me the secret handshake, and the hand signs they make, like this one."

Aimee formed her hands into a triangle, thumbs and forefingers touching. She regarded Marsh and Andy through the opening in middle.

"So much for secrecy," said Marsh.

"Daddy didn't like being told what to do; that's why he revealed the Masonic secrets to me, although frankly, they're sort of boring," Aimee said. She asked Marsh, "Didn't you join a secret society? I thought you were in Skull and Bones when you were at Yale."

"I went to Harvard. Surely you know that," Marsh said.

Aimee shrugged. "Did you? I guess they let anyone in." She liked annoying her brother by pretending to be unaware of his accomplishments.

"I don't know anything about the Skull and Bones Society, other than that their initiation ceremonies are said to be frightfully rowdy. I was in one of what are called the final clubs at Harvard, the Porcellian. About that, I will say only that I found the experience satisfactory," Marsh said.

"Then secret societies exist. It is as I thought," Andy said triumphantly.

"Harmless ones do, but not ones that go in for world domination," said Aimee.

Marsh considered Andy with a frown. "The question is, what are we going to do about you?"

"We swore a blood oath to come to each other's aid, should the need arise. I am here to save you from the Illuminati, whether you believe in them or not," Andy said.

"I don't recall swearing any blood oath."

"The dagger I gave you? Your gift to me of the miniature Statue of Liberty, from which issues a flame? Remember?"

"Yes, but I didn't think it was the same as a blood oath."

"Well, it was. At one time, the participants would have to slash themselves with the dagger, shake hands, and then go and hunt wild boar, on foot, armed only with a spear. You should be glad that the legendary and feared Ulakistani blood oath now involves nothing more than a simple exchange of gifts."

"I see," Marsh said. "In that case, you're welcome to stay here as long as you like, but who should we say you are?"

Andy smiled. "I have a brilliant idea."

CHAPTER TEN
ALOZ OLAK

The next morning, Marsh introduced Agent Burns to everyone who worked on the premises. She had already met the two maids, Janelle and Anea. Now she met Louetta Waites, the cook, and Lee, the butler, and about a dozen groundskeepers and gardeners, as well as Aloz Olak, Marsh's valet.

Marsh explained to the group gathered on the patio outside the kitchen that Aloz and Lee had worked together in Washington, D.C., at the embassy of the Republic of Korea. On Lee's recommendation, Marsh had hired Aloz to look after his extensive wardrobe.

"Thank the Lord," Janelle said fervently. "Do that mean me and Anea don't have to iron your shirts no more?"

Marsh agreed that's what it meant. He added that Aloz was originally from Slovenia.

Aimee, seizing the opportunity to annoy Marsh, asked, "Wasn't that where you were trapped in a cave one time, when you had to eat bugs and drink your own pee?"

Marsh gave her a sour look. "Yes, thanks for bringing that up."

Palmer and Trainor were still in bed. Jubilee, who had recovered from being nipped by Sheldon, the snapping turtle, was swimming in the pool, accompanied by Benjamin. The Olympic-size pool's azure water rippled in the sunlight as they splashed and shouted. Seamus, the Irish setter, ran along the edge, barking excitedly.

Aimee didn't usually get up this early. She'd agreed to be present at the 10 a.m. briefing in order to lend credibility to Marsh's story about the former dictator being his new valet.

Lee had agreed to confirm the story about the two of them having previously worked together. He provided Andy with two pairs of khaki trousers, a navy-blue blazer, and some starched white shirts, as well as a pair of Oxford shoes, and a tartan bow tie. It was what Lee wore when he was attending to his duties.

Seeing them together in their matching outfits, Louetta nodded approvingly. "This household is gettin' classy, like *Downton Abbey,* what with the butler and the valet dressed the same*."*

Anea and Janelle were sprawled in Adirondack chairs. Anea was painting her toenails red, while Janelle languidly applied lip gloss. Louetta told them, "You girls oughta wear black dresses with white aprons and little caps with ruffles on 'em. Class yourselves up, like professional members of a household staff, 'stead of lookin' like you fixin' to go on the rides at Six Flags."

Janelle gave a contemptuous laugh, to show that was never going to happen. "Here's an idea: why don't you class your own self up, and leave us alone?"

It was fiercely hot. In the gardens, the fountains splashed, sending up sparkling jets of water pumped in from the swamp at the rear of the property. In the distance, storm clouds the color of steel wool were bunched, promising rain and, with any luck, cooler temperatures.

The slate-paved patio where they were assembled at round tables under bright yellow canvas umbrellas, was surrounded on three sides by a neatly trimmed hedge of Leland cypress. Bees buzzed over lush beds of lavender, the silvery foliage and purple blossoms giving out a heady scent. A pair of terracotta planters filled with trailing vinca and pink impatiens stood beside the wood-framed screen door leading to the kitchen. Every few minutes, Louetta hustled inside and the screen door would slam shut behind her. She would reappear, smiling proudly, bearing another basket piled high with freshly baked pastries, along with carafes of coffee and freshly squeezed orange juice.

The cook was in her element. She loved feeding hungry people. The way the groundskeepers and gardeners were wolfing down her cinnamon rolls and blueberry crêpes delighted her. Like many gifted artists, she made what she did seem effortless. Louetta could have cooked for a battalion on a moment's notice with total aplomb.

No one seemed surprised by the presence of an FBI agent in their midst. Burns had explained she was there to inspect the house and surrounding property, and make suggestions for improving security. They all accepted that without question, as if there was nothing unusual in the FBI dropping by for a visit.

"Have you noticed anyone suspicious here lately?" she asked.

No, just the usual people from town who liked to visit the conservatories, and occasional tourists who had heard about the gardens at White Oaks. They wandered around, taking pictures and demanding to know where the restrooms were, and why there wasn't a gift shop.

"We considered charging admission and giving tours, the way they do at Magnolia Plantation in Charleston, but upon further reflection we decided we didn't want to bother," Marsh explained.

Yamma spoke up. "If you change your minds, I could come and help."

"That's okay, thanks for offering," Aimee said hastily. She feared they'd never get rid of the old lady as it was. *Marsh shouldn't have let her come here,* she thought, giving him a resentful look.

Yamma had risen early and explored the house and gardens. She'd only been there once before, shortly after her marriage to Courtland. She and Courtland's mother, Norma, hadn't gotten along and she'd never been invited back.

In a ground-floor room off a room devoted to storing sports equipment–croquet mallets, baseball gloves, water skis, tennis rackets, and other recreational paraphernalia belonging to generations of Trapnells–were shelves filled with vases. Yamma found several she fancied, including a bizarre object called a bird stump. It was two feet high, made from pearly white porcelain. It resembled a tree stump with truncated branches. There were openings in the top and sides in which to insert flowers. Porcelain ivy vines trailed around it, and here and there were porcelain forget-me-nots.

Yamma carefully lifted it down from the shelf. She would fill it with flowers from the garden and put it in the entry hall, where everyone could admire it.

The elderly lady had been lonely, living by herself. Being in a busy household cheered her up. There was much to see and do at White Oaks, and several ways she could make herself useful. One was never too old to be useful, she reminded herself. She only needed to find the right opportunity.

On the patio, the wind kicked up, rippling the scalloped edges of the umbrellas. Agent Burns thanked everyone for coming. She asked them to keep their eyes open and report to her if they saw anyone or anything suspicious.

Once inside, she went into the library and phoned her boss, Special Supervisory Agent Ronald DiFranco. He'd had a bad night, one filled with anxious dreams about missed appointments, and being lost in a maze of city streets, where everyone he encountered seemed to bear him ill-will. He had forgotten to wear his night guard, and as a result, his jaw ached. His voice was curt when he answered the phone.

"DiFranco," he barked, wincing as his jaw gave a painful twinge. "God damn it, speak up,' he snarled, although Burns hadn't said anything yet.

"Everything's quiet here, sir," Burns told him. "No strangers reported, nothing suspicious. The people employed here are just ordinary country folk, except for two who used to work at one of the embassies in Washington. They'd have to have had security clearances and passed a background check. The family's here, too, most of them. One of them is a Buddhist nun. She's not here; she's at a monastery in Mississippi."

"A Buddhist nun? In Mississippi? Jesus Christ! Which one is she?"

"Karen Trapnell, sir. She's Blanton Trapnell's daughter by his first wife."

"What kind of American becomes a Buddhist nun? All the Trapnells are crazy, aren't they?"

"Probably, sir."

DiFranco massaged his aching jaw. "At least we don't have to worry about that lunatic in Texas, that deposed dictator from a country nobody ever heard of. We believe the two hired guns who were shot in Blue Ridge were after him. They must have had bad info. He's in no danger; the Secret Service is guarding him. They have it under control."

After he fled Ulakistan, Andy had been offered sanctuary by the president of the United States, who was enticed by the vast wealth Andy had managed to smuggle out of his country. That president had been succeeded by another, one uninterested in getting his hands on Andy's loot. Andy's current status hovered somewhere between that of an honored guest and a prisoner under house arrest.

What DiFranco didn't know, what not even the director of the FBI knew, due to internecine warfare between the various government agencies, was that Andy had eluded his Secret Service minders and was on the loose.

The FBI disliked the Secret Service and vice versa, in the same way state police dislike local police, and the U.S. Marshals dislike the state police, and agents of the Treasury Department dislike those from the Department of Homeland Security, who in turn dislike the Transportation Security Administration and the Immigration and Naturalization Service. It had always been that way, this chain of suspicion and jealous hoarding of information. As each new department was created, it, in turn, viewed all the others with thinly veiled enmity and disdain.

The Secret Service was frantically searching for Andy, without letting any other law-enforcement agency, either local, state, or federal, know he was missing. That was working about as well as could be expected. They were currently following a tip that reported him being sighted at a campground in Oklahoma. Meanwhile, he was upstairs at White Oaks, admiring Marsh's collection of luxury timepieces.

"What're they like, the family? They're filthy rich, aren't they?" DiFranco asked Burns.

"There's a vintage Rolls-Royce parked out front, and they have a Picasso."

"Those bastards!" DiFranco cried, anguished by the unfairness of it all. "None of them work, except for Marsh Trapnell, and we all know what *he* does, the little pipsqueak. The rest of them live off trust funds, like parasites."

"The sister works, the one that's not a Buddhist nun. She's Aimee Trapnell, the fashion designer," said Burns.

"That's not work," DiFranco scoffed. "It's not a real job. She's just a socialite who fools around designing clothes. And she's got all those snakes. What kind of woman has all those snakes?"

DiFranco's wife had showed him a magazine article about Aimee and her serpents. It was titled "Snake Eyes," and featured a closeup of Aimee's eerie green eyes.

"I don't know, sir. I suppose she likes them," Burns said.

"Snakes are creepy," DiFranco said decisively. "What about the brother, the other one, the one who's not a scumbag arms dealer?"

"Trainor Trapnell is what I guess you'd call a good old boy," Burns said. "He and his wife built a giant freestanding replica of the *Titanic* in Decatur. People buy tickets to go inside. It shudders, as if it hit an iceberg, then it leans over, and everyone tries to escape."

There was an astonished silence as DiFranco took that in. Then he said, "It sounds dangerous. Why would they build something dangerous like that?"

"I don't know, sir. Trainor Trapnell and his wife have a little girl. They're all here. The only other family members here are an old aunt and Aimee Trapnell's teenage son. He seems like a normal kid."

"None of them are normal," DiFranco said morosely. "What's the house like, pretty fancy?"

Burns looked around the library. It was a condensed version of the Rose Main Reading Room at the New York Public Library, one of the most beautiful public rooms in North America. On the high ceiling, what at first appeared to be a skylight was a trompe l'oeil mural of a cerulean sky, framed by puffy white clouds. Glass-topped display cases held rare volumes, including a Bible published in 1535 by Myles Coverdale, the first Bible printed in English.

"Pretty fancy," she agreed.

Burns had been stunned when Marsh showed her the library. There had to be at least five thousand books in there. She asked if his father had liked to read.

Marsh quirked an amused eyebrow. "Daddy? Read? Whatever gave you that idea?"

"You said he collected all these books." She waved her hand to indicate the book-filled stacks climbing to the ceiling.

"I don't believe Daddy ever read a book in his entire life, aside from what they made him read in school." Marsh nodded at display cases containing four massive "double elephant" volumes of John James Audubon's *The Birds of America*. "These are investments. Daddy had rare book dealers in New York, London, and Paris looking out for acquisitions for him. They made some extraordinary finds."

Burns scanned the ceiling, relieved to make out a fire suppression system disguised in some of the plaster rosettes. That was good. She hated to think of this irreplaceable collection going up in flames. "Do you have motion sensors in here? Alarms of any kind?"

"No, and before you ask, we don't have them anywhere at White Oaks. Daddy said they were too much trouble, always going off when they weren't supposed to. I don't think Louetta would like having to deal with key pads. They'd only fluster her. She's always forgetting her password and getting locked out of the computer in the kitchen."

Burns realized she was fighting a losing battle. "It's up to you, but I think it's a miracle you've never been robbed."

"Robbing us would be unwise," Marsh said.

Something in the way he said it chilled Burns to her core.

CHAPTER ELEVEN
AIMEE GOES SNOOPING

The rain held off until shortly before noon, when the storm broke overhead with a blinding flash of lightning, followed by a roar of thunder. The old mansion shuddered. Aimee, rushing inside from the balcony outside her bedroom where she'd been sunbathing, noticed the French door to the balcony next door was open. It belonged to the room where Yamma was staying.

Aimee threw on a robe and went and tapped on the door. When there was no response, she went in.

The bed was neatly made. There was no sign of Yamma. Rain was pouring in, and Aimee closed the balcony door, tsk-tsking at the wet carpet. A suitcase on a luggage stand caught her eye. It was just like Yamma, she thought, to have an old-fashioned suitcase, one which had to be lifted by a handle and lugged around, instead of the rolling kind. Aimee studied it, frowning, then looked at the open door leading to the corridor. She could hear the whine of a vacuum cleaner, but there was no sign of anyone. From upstairs came pounding footsteps, as Jubilee and Benjamin played some kind of game.

Aimee closed the door, then went back to studying the suitcase. It was shut, its shiny brass latches fastened. Was it locked? Aimee decided to find out. She doubted the old lady had anything interesting in there, but Aimee had always been beset by curiosity. Like Rikki-Tikki-Tavi, the inquisitive mongoose in Rudyard Kipling's *The Jungle Book,* her motto was "Run and find out."

Five minutes later, Aimee found Marsh in their father's old office. Aimee had on a full-skirted sundress of her own design. Its fabric was printed with what appeared to be pastel-colored jelly beans with spindly, spiderlike legs. In fact, they were a representation of the Yersinia pestis bacteria, better known as the bubonic plague. Around the hem were what at first glance were brambles, but upon closer examination proved to be a parade of rats.

Her outfit included thick-soled, hot-pink vinyl boots, with hideous, grimacing green faces on the toes. This was classic Clobber. Admirers of Aimee's brand agreed there was no one to compare with her for style.

The office was as extraordinary in its own way as the Gentlemen's Parlor and the library. While those were awe-inspiring, Blanton's office looked as though it belonged in a rundown used car dealership, which is precisely where it originated.

The battered metal desk, rusted metal filing cabinets, and worn indoor-outdoor carpeting were relics of a used car dealership, the first business Blanton acquired after graduating from the University of Georgia. That humble beginning set him on the path to becoming a billionaire. He moved the contents to White Oaks, as a symbol of how far he had come.

Breathlessly, Aimee announced, "You won't believe what Yamma has in her suitcase."

Marsh had his feet up on the desk. He was reading the *Pontahatcha Times-Observer,* a weekly broadsheet tasked with reporting the news from the neighboring town of Pontahatcha.

"Listen to this," Marsh said, and read aloud: "There was considerable excitement Friday night when a varmint got into Eula Stipple's vegetable garden and tore it up. Junior Stipple swears it was Bigfoot. He shared this image with our editorial staff, taken from his deer cam, of what he claims is the mysterious and elusive cryptid."

Marsh lowered the paper and regarded his sister with a grin. "It's front-page news, along with the photo. It could be anything, really, but my guess is it's a bear. The other big news is that Jennifer Ralston, daughter of Eubanks and Melody Ralston, discovered a two-foot-long iguana in her car as she was on her way to work as assistant produce manager at the Piggly Wiggly."

Reading aloud, he said, "The reptile made its presence known as Ms. Ralston approached the intersection of Old Bucksaw Road and Jefferson Davis Drive. Ms. Ralston remained calm. With remarkable presence of mind, she activated her hazard signal, threw open the door, and prodded the beast with an umbrella, causing it to exit the vehicle. It ran off in the direction of Chet Moffat's truck patch."

Aimee appeared unimpressed by this masterpiece of local journalism. Marsh went on, "There's a sidebar consisting of an interview with someone with the wonderful name of Bartholomew Bimber. He owns an iguana. He says the one in Ms. Ralson's car was probably an escaped pet, and that she should have called animal control instead of poking it with an umbrella. I see trouble ahead, as people take sides and weigh in on the best way to deal with finding an iguana in one's vehicle. It could get ugly. What do you think?"

Aimee said, "I don't give a hoot about Bartholomew Bimber, or any of those idiots in Pontahatcha. Yamma has a gun."

Marsh put the paper down. "What are you talking about?"

"You know how Yamma said she was afraid of guns and would never own one?"

Marsh looked thoughtful. "I recall her saying that."

"Well, she lied," Aimee said triumphantly. "She has a gun. It's upstairs right now. It's in her suitcase. I saw it."

"Why were you going through her suitcase?"

"I went in to close the door to the balcony. Rain was pouring in. Her suitcase was there so I just..." She trailed off, embarrassed.

"Snooped. You snooped through her belongings."

"I thought I'd see if I could help by putting her things away for her," Aimee said, refusing to meet Marsh's eyes.

Marsh swung his feet off the desk. "It doesn't necessarily mean anything. She has a right to have a gun."

"But why did she lie about it? And why would she bring it to White Oaks?"

"Maybe she forgot it was in her suitcase."

"It was right on top. She must have put it in after she packed her clothes and things."

Marsh rubbed his chin. "She packed her bag when Dooley paid her bail and drove her down here, is that right?"

"I guess so."

"Then Dooley could have given it to her. What kind of gun was it?"

"Does it matter?"

"It could be a toy, a water pistol, something for Jubilee."

"It's not a toy. I know a real gun when I see one. It was a 9mm Ruger with fixed sights. It was loaded; I checked. I know what kind of gun it was because you gave me one just like it."

Aimee was resentful that Marsh would think she would confuse a child's toy with a deadly weapon. "Why would Dooley give it to her to bring to White Oaks? It's not as if it he thought it would make a good hostess gift. A bottle of wine is a hostess gift. A scented candle is a hostess gift. A gun is not a hostess gift. I say we confront her and demand to know what she's doing with it."

Marsh vetoed that idea. "She's an old lady. She's been through a lot. Finding two bodies, then being questioned by the police, that would be enough to rattle anyone. Perhaps the gun belonged to her late husband. She could have been in shock when she packed her bag, and put it in there without thinking. Questioning her about it would be rude. She is our guest, after all. Please, don't bring it up."

"All right, if you say so, but I'm going to keep an eye on her."

At that moment Andy entered the office. He told Marsh, "I have polished your shoes, like a good valet. Lee asked me to tell you it is time for luncheon."

Addressing Aimee, he said, "You look especially beautiful today, Miss Aimee. I hope you are considering my offer of making you first lady of the glorious nation of Ulakistan."

Aimee was not attracted to the Madman of the Steppes. However, the thought of being first lady was tempting. She said she was thinking about it.

"Playing hard to get, eh? I like that," Andy said. "How about if I throw in a diamond tiara for you to wear on state occasions?"

"I already have some extremely valuable diamond jewelry, given to me by my late husband, the margrave," Aimee said haughtily. "It's a matched set, a necklace, a brooch, and a bracelet that belonged to Empress Maria Theresa. The centerpiece of the necklace is a flawless green diamond. It's huge; it weighs four hundred and eight carats."

If Andy was impressed, he didn't let on. "Bah, that is nothing. I can give you a larger diamond than that, any color you like, just say you will marry me."

"I'll think about it," Aimee said. "Now I want lunch. Marsh, are you coming?"

Andy took her hand and raised it to his mouth, gazing soulfully into her eyes, stopping just short of brushing his lips against her knuckles. "The rain is letting up. I shall go for a stroll in the grounds, and think about how beautiful your official portrait will be, hanging in a prominent place in the Presidential Palace, with you ablaze in diamonds."

CHAPTER TWELVE
BABY PATTY CAKE AGAIN

Luncheon was served in the breakfast room. It was a cheerful room, with pistachio-green walls, white wicker furniture, and large windows overlooking the patio. The rain had slowed to a drizzle.

"This is just a little bite to hold y'all over until dinner," Louetta said, bringing in plate after steaming plate of food. The "little bite" consisted of crab bisque, shrimp and grits with andouille sausage and wild mushrooms, cornbread, okra, fried green tomatoes, and a choice of caramel cake or banana pudding for dessert.

Trainor set in to making it disappear as fast as possible.

In the adjoining kitchen, a radio was playing the title track from Baby Patty Cake's album, *THOT.* Janelle and Anea had the volume turned up, and every word could be plainly heard in the breakfast room.

The chorus went, *"Who that ho? Everybody know. Everybody know that she a ho."*

"What a lively tune!" said Yamma.

Jubilee's forehead wrinkled in puzzlement. "What's a ho?"

Nobody wanted to answer. Palmer took her time buttering a piece of cornbread, trying to think how to respond. Finally, she said, "It's a very friendly lady."

"When I grow up, I'm going to be a ho," Jubilee said.

Benjamin snickered.

"No, you're not," said Trainor, spooning a large helping of shrimp and grits onto his plate and liberally dousing it with hot sauce.

Jubilee stuck out her lower lip. "Yes, I am. I'm going to be the biggest ho in the whole world, so there."

"Don't talk to your daddy that way," Louetta scolded her. Raising her voice, she called into the kitchen, "Girls, cut that noise off. There's a child listening."

Anea called back, unwisely, as it turned out, "There's nothing wrong with this song. Baby Patty Cake is smart. She know what's going on. On her Instagram she talk about the new world order and the lizard people and the Illuminati and a lot of important stuff that the mainstream media don't cover. You old-fashioned. You out of touch."

"Keep that sass up, and you 'bout to get an old-fashioned surprise," the cook replied, storming into the kitchen.

As the door swung shut, the Trapnells and Agent Burns heard Janelle tell Anea, "Now you done it. She gonna kick your ass."

Palmer thought it best to change the subject. "Guess what! I've been accepted into the Daughters of Arsinoe. Dorcas Snipes, the exalted worthy matron, phoned this morning. I'm in!"

"Congratulations, Chicken Legs," Trainor said, relieved that his wife's tears and tantrums over her fear of being blackballed were over.

"Yes, congratulations," echoed Agent Burns. She had never heard of the Daughters of Arsinoe. She hoped it wasn't a white supremacist organization.

"Chandler is going to be furious. This is going to just about kill her," Palmer said happily, thinking of how her friend would react, once she learned Palmer would be a member.

"You were worried over nothing," Aimee told her.

"I know," Palmer agreed. "I remembered how proud Dorcas Snipes is of her ancestors. One of them was a lady archeologist. She went to Egypt and wrote a book about all the old tombs and mummies and things they dug up. She made friends with an English lady there, a Mrs. Mallowan. She wrote the introduction to the book, Mrs. Mallowan, I mean. I guess it wasn't a very good book because there were only twenty copies printed. There's one in the library here, can you believe it? I told Mrs. Snipes I'd give it to her. That's when she said I can be a Daughter of Arsinoe."

Agent Burns stopped eating. "You said the introduction was written by a Mrs. Mallowan?"

"Mrs. Max Mallowan. Why?"

Burns put down her spoon. "That's Agatha Christie."

"Just imagine!" Yamma exclaimed. "I've read all of her books. It was ingenious, the way she didn't reveal the murderer's identity until the end, and then there it was, as clear as day, if you'd only put the right clues together."

"I believe you're correct. Agatha Christie's second husband was an archeologist. As I recall, his surname was Mallowan." Marsh shook his head in amazement. "There were only twenty copies? That book must be worth a fortune. It should remain here, as part of the collection."

Palmer's mouth fell open in dismay. "No! That's not fair! I found it. I looked through the catalogue of books that Blanton had made up and there it was: *Treasures of the Pharaohs: Discoveries in the Valley of the Kings,* by Olive Snipes, with a foreword by Mrs. Max Mallowan."

She aimed a poisonous glare at Marsh. "I found it, and I'm giving it to Dorcas Snipes. There are plenty of books in the library. I have a right to give one away, if it gets me into the Daughters of Arsinoe." She turned to her husband and implored, "Tell him, Trainor! Tell him I can have it."

Trainor looked longingly at the bowl of banana pudding, his favorite dessert, as Louetta had announced when she brought it in and placed it on the table where they all sat, waiting to hear what Trainor would say. He pleaded, "Come on, Marsh. It's just one little book."

"We've been through this before, when you wanted Daddy's Rolls-Royce, and some of the paintings. We can't start taking things from White Oaks, willy-nilly. Have the book appraised, and then ask Daddy's lawyer what you should do."

"Bingo Sparks is senile. I can't believe they still let him practice," Aimee said of the old attorney. "He'd take forever to decide, and then he'd forget what the question was. You should resolve it the way you always used to settle disputes between the two of you."

A gleam came into Marsh's eyes. "Good idea. I'm game if he is."

"You're on!" said Trainor, throwing down his napkin. "We'll have a duel."

Marsh pushed back his chair and rose to his full height of five feet, four inches. He asked Trainor, "Are you sure that's the way you want it?"

Trainor rose and faced his brother across the table. "Let's do this."

"Very well," said Marsh, flexing his shoulders. "On my count. One, two, three, shoot!"

Trainor won the game of rock paper scissors and Marsh graciously conceded defeat. Palmer squealed and flung her arms around Trainor's neck. "Thank you, Boo Bear! You're my knight in shining armor!"

"The rain has stopped," Yamma observed, looking out onto the patio. Through the gap in the hedge, Marsh's valet could be seen walking in the distance. Yamma rose from her seat, "I'm going for a stroll in the garden. It will help settle my digestion after all this excitement."

CHAPTER THIRTEEN
DISASTER AVERTED

Odell Purvey, one of the gardeners at White Oaks, was shoveling mulch onto a flower bed when something plummeted from the top of the sixty-foot-tall observation tower overlooking the gardens and the tangled vegetation of the swamp at the rear of the property. A heavy stone landed with a thud, kicking up a spray of mulch and narrowly missing Odell. Looking up, he saw two figures struggling atop the tower, where one of the large upright stones forming a battlement was now missing.

"Hang on, I'm coming!" Odell shouted. He sprinted to the tower, running through flower beds, and trampling flowers in his haste. Once inside, he hurried up the winding stairs, breathing hard, the soles of his boots slapping on the stone steps. At the top, he found Yamma collapsed on the floor. Marsh's valet stood over her, white-faced and trembling.

"We nearly went over," he told Odell. "A stone was loose. I was admiring the view when this lady came up."

"I'm afraid I became dizzy and stumbled into this nice young man," Yamma said apologetically, as Odell helped her to her feet.

"Best to close this tower until it can be inspected for safety. I shall inform my employer," Andy said, and set off toward the house.

"A true gentleman's gentleman," Yamma murmured, watching his retreating navy-blue jacketed back. "I don't know what would have happened if he hadn't been there. Gracious! I might have fallen off."

Andy found Marsh in a ground-floor room. It had dark wood wainscoting and resembled an Edwardian-era club room, furnished with a well-stocked bar and comfortable leather armchairs with nail-head trim. At one end of the room the antique Tabriz carpet gave way, jarringly, to wall-to-wall in lurid neon colors, depicting Sonic the Hedgehog and Bart Simpson capering beneath a bank of classic video arcade machines. These were gifts to Trainor from his father, to encourage him to put his nose to the grindstone and graduate from high school, something Trainor had showed signs of being unable or unwilling to accomplish.

Marsh and Trainor were playing pool on an antique table, an artifact from a New Orleans hotel that went bust during the Depression.

"I think someone tried to kill me," Andy told Marsh.

Trainor lined up a shot, concentrating fiercely, eyes narrowed, tongue protruding between his teeth. "You're jokin'. Nobody kills valets. Who'd wanna bother? No offense, Aloz."

"Aloz has a Slavic soul. He always imagines the worst," Marsh said lightly. Placing his cue in the rack, he told the ersatz valet, "Come upstairs with me. I could use your help in selecting a tuxedo to wear to dinner tonight."

"You got more than one tuxedo? I should of known, the way you dress so fancy. I only got one, but it's a good one. It's made out of velvet, in a color they call salmon, like the fish. I was married in it, three times," Trainor said.

"I recall it well," Marsh said, suppressing a shudder at the memory of his brother's garish pinkish-orange tuxedo.

In Marsh's room, Andy paced distractedly, his face a mask of anxiety. Marsh seated himself at the rolltop desk. He folded his arms and waited for Andy to speak.

"Your aunt bumped me as I was leaning over the edge of the tower in the garden. I think she intended to do it. One of the big stones came loose and fell to the ground," Andy said.

"Go on," said Marsh. He thought of the gun Aimee said she had seen in Yamma's suitcase. If the old lady had wanted to kill Andy, she could have lured him into the swamp and shot him, where no one could see. Pushing him off the tower was too risky, with so many potential witnesses. And why would Yamma want to harm Andy? She didn't even know him. It made no sense.

"I thought I was alone," Andy said. "I didn't hear her approach. She said nothing, only bumped. When I did not fall, she seized me. She is strong for an old woman."

Marsh watched him, saying nothing.

"My friend, I am troubled by this. Could the big stone have been loosened deliberately?"

"It's possible, but unlikely. That tower is over a thousand years old. My grandmother, the lady who designed the gardens, had it brought over from Ireland. It was taken apart, stone by stone, shipped here, and reassembled. She was always embarking on ambitious projects like that. She was an unusual woman. She lived to be almost one hundred and four years old. I was too young to remember her, but Trainor claims he does. He says he was terrified of her."

"Are you saying the stone fell accidentally? My friend, I do not believe in accidents," Andy said.

"The tower was put up here before the Second World War. Cement deteriorates in this hot, moist climate. I'm surprised a stone didn't fall off sooner. It's fortunate no one was injured."

Andy was unconvinced. "Perhaps, but why did your aunt not speak when she found me atop the tower? Why did she only bump, like this?" He thrust out his hip to demonstrate.

"She could have lost her balance. As to why she didn't speak to you, I can't say. We get the occasional tourist visiting the grounds. She could have mistaken you for one at first and been shy about speaking. Don't worry about it. There's no reason why Yamma would want to harm you, or anyone. The important thing is you're all right. Here, have one of these."

Marsh opened a desk drawer and took out a bag of soft caramels, individually wrapped in striped green, white, and black waxed paper.

"Freyju karamellur. They're from Iceland. I have a friend who lives there," he said. "You'd like her; you have something in common. Both of you were forced to leave your respective countries suddenly, under unpleasant circumstances."

Unwrapping a piece, Andy said, "Something was not right about that tower business. Oh! This candy is good!"

"Keep the bag; I have plenty more," Marsh said. "Relax, you're safe here. No one knows who you are, except for me, and Lee, and Aimee. What could go wrong?"

CHAPTER FOURTEEN
THE INSTRUMENT ROOM

Palmer had her bags packed, anxious to give the book to Dorcas Snipes and secure her membership in the Daughters of Arsinoe. She was ready for action, dressed in a white cotton halter top and brown-and-white striped drawstring linen trousers. A silk Hermès scarf was knotted, kerchief-style, under her chin.

Agent Burns encountered her in the entry hall. Surprised, she said, "You're not leaving?

"I need to get back to Atlanta. Trainor and Jubilee will be staying a little longer."

This was unexpected. Burns had thought everyone would stay put until she had permission from DiFranco to let them leave. "You can't go. It might not be safe. The deaths of those two men are still being investigated."

"They had nothing to do with me. I don't associate with criminals," Palmer snapped as she rolled her suitcase toward the front door, eager to make her escape.

Hearing their voices, Lee came into the entry hall from the Gentlemen's Parlor, where he had been dusting the statues. Sensing tension in the air, he looked back and forth between the two women, trying to figure out what was going on.

"Are you leaving us, Mrs. Trapnell?" he asked.

"That's right. My husband and our daughter will be staying a while longer. Help me put my things in the BMW. My husband can drive the Rolls to Atlanta."

Dismayed, Lee looked to Agent Burns for guidance. The Rolls-Royce was supposed to remain at White Oaks. "I can call you an Uber, or perhaps one of the staff could drive you."

Palmer nixed that idea. "Don't be silly. I'm perfectly capable of driving myself." She hoisted the strap of her Louis Vuitton backpack higher on her shoulder and trundled the suitcase closer to the door. "Get that garment bag, would you?"

"I have orders to keep all of you here, for your own protection," Burns said, knowing she couldn't force Palmer to stay if she was determined to leave.

Palmer let out an exasperated sigh. She told Lee, "Give her some money, so she lets me leave. I'll pay you back."

Burns couldn't believe her ears. "It's against the law to attempt to bribe a federal agent."

"I'm not; I told him to do it," Palmer said.

At that moment, the front door opened and Marsh came in. "I have bad news," he announced. "Someone slashed the tires on Trainor's BMW."

"Then I'll take the Rolls to Atlanta," Palmer said.

Marsh shook his head, his gray eyes glacial. "Not without the keys you're not, and I'm not giving them to you. Daddy's Rolls-Royce stays here. That was the agreement. Wait until Agent Burns says you can leave, then I'll have new tires put on the BMW and drive you to Atlanta myself."

Frustrated, Palmer kicked the garment bag, sending it skidding across the polished marble floor. It hit Seamus' basket, where the dog was sleeping. He leapt to his feet, aggravated at having his nap disturbed.

"I hate you, Marsh," Palmer fumed.

Marsh regarded her calmly. "If I were you, I'd hate whoever slashed your tires. Acts of senseless vandalism occur occasionally, I'm sorry to say, even in rural communities like Cobbs."

"I don't give a crap. I'm going to Atlanta and nobody's going to stop me," Palmer declared, her eyes wild. She sounded for all the world like Scarlett O'Hara, when she vowed that as God was her witness, she would never be hungry again. She shouted, "Trainor! Where are you? Marsh is being ugly. He won't let me have the Rolls."

Unperturbed, Marsh went to the bird stump and began rearranging the flowers Yamma had put in it. "There's another solution, rather than you tearing off to Atlanta in a vintage Rolls-Royce that you don't know how to operate properly."

Palmer hesitated. It was true. She didn't know how to drive a vehicle with a manual transmission. Not only that, the steering wheel of the Rolls was located, disconcertingly, on the right.

Marsh suggested, "If you're hot to trot to get that book to Dorcas Snipes, why not let me drive you to the UPS store in Pontahatcha? You can arrange to have it sent so she has it by this afternoon. I take it your presence isn't required at this time, just the book's?"

Palmer grudgingly admitted, "Yes, just the book."

"In that case, once Mrs. Snipes has it in her possession, voilà! You're in with the in crowd."

Instantly, Palmer was all smiles. "That's a good idea, Marsh. You're a genius."

Marsh broke off a white gardenia blossom and tucked it behind his ear. "I appreciate the compliment, but I'm too modest to confirm it."

Crisis averted, Agent Burns excused herself and went to call DiFranco. A closet-sized space between the library and Blanton's office had, long ago, been dubbed the Instrument Room. "The Instrument" was what Blanton's father, Moxley Trapnell, called the telephone when it was a brand-new invention.

Moxley's candlestick telephone was the first one in Cobbs. Its installation created a panic among the townspeople. They feared that being in its proximity could cause madness, either that or the electricity running through the telephone line might "go bad" and fry them to cinders.

The Instrument initially served as a means of communication between White Oaks and the fertilizer factory, an odiferous but profitable business which Moxley owned. Its reach later expanded to connect it with all Moxley's businesses, as well as the homes of his managers and certain favored citizens, such as the mayor and the sheriff and the doctor.

Agent Burns went into the Instrument Room and closed the door. The walls and ceiling were completely papered in Confederate currency. Moxley, while clinging to the hope that the South would rise again, doubted the bills would ever be worth more than the paper they were printed on. He pasted them up in the Instrument Room as a salute to the Lost Cause.

A triangular bench built into one corner was upholstered in cracked green leather. Burns sat and took out her phone. She made a face at a one-hundred-dollar bill pasted on the wall to her right. It depicted an agrarian scene of slaves picking cotton, appearing placidly content with their lot in life. Burns rolled her eyes and called DiFranco.

He answered on the first ring. His jaw no longer ached, the result of his having worn his night guard the night before. He was in an exuberant mood. The SAC had praised a memo DiFranco wrote about diversity training.

"Well done, DiFranco," McClung, the Special Agent in Charge of the Atlanta field office had said. DiFranco kept repeating those words in his head, as amazed and flattered as a mousy high school girl who's been singled out for a compliment from the homecoming queen. *Well done, DiFranco.* The thought of those words made him walk taller and hold his head higher.

"How goes it, Agent Burns?" he asked, chipper as a chickadee.

"Palmer Trapnell was about to leave, sir, but someone slashed her tires," she said.

"Well done." DiFranco felt a glow of satisfaction at repeating the SAC's words to one of his own subordinates.

Incredulous, Burns sputtered, "What? No! I didn't do it."

"Sure, you didn't," DiFranco chuckled, clearly believing otherwise. "I get it; you can't be too careful, in case someone's listening. Slashing her tires shows initiative on your part."

"I really didn't do it," Burns insisted. Was DiFranco praising her for committing vandalism? Despite the air-conditioning, sweat beaded her forehead. It was claustrophobic in that little room, surrounded by all that useless money. Confederate currency, she realized, was pocket-sized propaganda, with images of slaves working in fields next to those of mythological Greek gods and goddesses. It implied that slavery was right and just, and would continue forever, sanctioned by law.

The notes weren't backed by gold or silver, and had no guaranteed value. That was all right, the optimistic Southerners decided. When the South eventually triumphed, as it surely would, then the bearers would be paid.

Foolish, thought Burns. She asked DiFranco, "When can I tell everyone they can leave?"

"Soon, soon, we'll give it a few more days," he assured her.

DiFranco was only guessing. His superiors had told him nothing, one way or the other. They themselves knew nothing, and they preferred not to make inquiries of the secretive, powerful, government agency which had given the FBI its orders regarding keeping the Trapnells at White Oaks. It was best not to ask in case the question was seen as impertinent. The FBI was terribly afraid of that agency. Any communication from it caused waves of panic to thrum throughout the bureau. Best to ask no questions and wait for it to make its intentions clear.

"Yes, sir," Burns said.

"In the meantime, enjoy yourself," DiFranco said expansively. "Consider it a sort of paid vacation. Have fun. Just be sure and keep an eye on Marsh Trapnell. He's a slippery one, always up to something. Goodbye!" DiFranco ended the call.

Agent Burns unwrapped the hair tie holding her bun in place. Her hair fell to her shoulders, straight and shining, black as a pool of ink. It looked like she was going to be stuck at White Oaks for the foreseeable future.

She exited the Instrument Room to find Marsh loitering in the entry hall. His collarless shirt was unbuttoned, and his hands were in the pockets of his board shorts. He said, "I don't get back here often. When I'm away, I like to think of White Oaks being here, unchanged, the way it has always been." He looked keenly at her and asked, "Is all well, Agent Burns?"

Burns twisted her hair back into a bun. "My supervisor thinks I slashed the tires on your brother's car."

"I'm certain you didn't."

"How can you be so sure?"

"Because I did."

"Come on, be serious."

"I am serious. I slashed the tires with my dagger in order to prevent Palmer from hot-footing it off to Atlanta with that book she's so excited about. I saw no reason for her to be there in person to present it to the exulted high priestess in charge of the Daughters of Arson, or whatever it's called, so..." He made slashing motions in the air. "I did it to help you."

"Sweet disco-dancing Jesus! You carry a dagger?"

"Doesn't everyone? A friend gave it to me." Marsh lifted his shirt and withdrew the dagger Andy gave him from a leather sheath on his belt. The rubies glittered cruelly under the light of the chandelier as he extended it, handle-first, toward Burns.

"That's a dagger, all right. Are those real rubies?"

"Of course. Giving someone a weapon encrusted with fake gems would be gauche, don't you think?

"I'm not really up on that sort of thing," Burns admitted. "More to the point, how does slashing your sister-in-law's tires help me?"

Marsh tucked the wickedly sharp blade back into its sheath and gazed serenely at her. "You wanted us all to remain here, and now we shall. I'll see to it that the book is delivered posthaste to the lady in Atlanta. I promised Palmer a new set of tires and I mean to keep my word, but not until you say we can leave."

Burns didn't know how to respond. Those high-performance tires had to cost at least five hundred dollars apiece. That was pocket change to Marsh, but still, it was a gallant gesture for him to make on her behalf.

Couldn't he simply have offered to drive Palmer to the UPS store in the first place, without destroying the tires? Palmer might have refused, preferring to deliver the book to Mrs. Snipes in person and bask in her gratitude. Marsh wasn't taking any chances. Never one to be constrained by convention, he had employed an extreme method to prevent that from happening.

"Thanks, I guess."

"You're welcome. I was happy to assist my partner."

"We're not partners, Bad Choices."

"Perhaps not in an official capacity, but I like to think we have a special bond."

"It's special, all right. Where is everyone?"

There was no one else in sight. Their voices echoed in the high-ceilinged space.

Marsh gave Burns a teasing grin. "Are you asking for the whereabouts of everyone in the world, or just everyone in this household?"

"Everyone here."

"Palmer's upstairs. So is Aimee. They're whitening their teeth, or exfoliating their legs, or whatever personal upkeep they perform when they have some spare moments; self-care, I believe it's called. Yamma's upstairs, too, taking a nap. Lee and Aloz are in the butler's pantry. They're polishing the silver, in preparation for dinner tonight in the dining room. Louetta likes it when we dine formally, in the dining room. She's in the kitchen. She's got Janelle and Anea helping her make an amuse-bouche for us to sample before the first course."

Burns made a mental head count. "Where's your brother and his little girl? Where's your nephew?"

"Ah," said Marsh. "I was getting to them. They're outside, swimming. It's a beautiful day. We should join them and get some fresh air and exercise. Did you remember to pack your government-sanctioned bathing attire?"

"I'm not here to go swimming, so no, I didn't bring a bathing suit."

"All work and no play make Carson Burns a dull FBI agent," Marsh said sorrowfully. Then he winked. "Fortunately, we have an array of bathing suits out back, in the pool house, all styles and sizes. We'll get you into one and then we'll go swimming. Unless you don't know how."

Marsh's sparkling eyes were the deep gray of antique pewter. Burns recalled reading somewhere that true gray eye color was extremely rare. Her own eyes, a rich brown, were the most common color, shared by almost eighty percent of the world's population, followed by blue. Aimee's neon-green eyes were unusual. Only about two percent of the population had green eyes, the percentage higher among those of Celtic or Germanic ancestry. Rarest of all were naturally gray eyes, like Marsh's. It was a trait which appeared in less than one percent of the human population.

Nettled by Marsh's jibe about her not knowing how to swim, Burns rose to the challenge. "I was on the swim team in college. I can probably swim better than you."

Marsh clapped his hands. "Excellent! Aquatic adventures await. Off we go!"

CHAPTER FIFTEEN
POISONED PUDDING

Marsh and Agent Burns walked through the house and out onto the patio, where they were met by a frantic Benjamin. He ran toward them, his feet bare, his hair and bathing suit dripping wet. His face contorted in panic, he cried, "Something's wrong with Uncle Trainor and Jubilee! Call an ambulance!"

"Are they in the pool?" asked Marsh, fearing they had drowned.

"No, they're on the ground next to the pool. They were throwing up and now Jubilee's unconscious and Uncle Trainor's having a seizure. It's bad. Call an ambulance!"

An ambulance arrived and took Trainor and Jubilee to the hospital in Pontahatcha. Marsh and Palmer followed in the Rolls-Royce. A sheriff's deputy, a short, pudgy woman named Gloria Beth Hoopsinger, had accompanied the ambulance to White Oaks in a patrol car. Hoopsinger remained behind with Agent Burns. She was both intimidated and thrilled at being in the presence of an FBI agent.

The swimming pool had gone from being a scene of chaos to one of aftermath. Wet towels were crumpled on the concrete deck, amid puddles of vomit. Two of the lounge chairs were overturned.

Hoopsinger walked carefully, avoiding the vomit. She pulled on a pair of black, law enforcement, powder-free nitrile gloves and bent down to pick up two plastic spoons and two plastic cups. One of the cups was empty, the other was half-full of a yellow substance resembling custard.

She sniffed the cup, then placed both cups and spoons in separate evidence bags. She told Agent Burns, "Smells like banana pudding, ma'am, although we won't know for certain until the results come back from the lab."

Hoopsinger thought she sounded properly official, although she wasn't sure where such a lab might be that could confirm or deny the presence of banana pudding. Maybe someone at the state police barracks on the highway outside of Pontahatcha would know.

Benjamin spoke up, "It *is* banana pudding."

Hoopsinger frowned, displeased by this civilian butting in to her investigation. "How do you know?"

"Because Uncle Trainor said so. We were swimming and he got hungry, so he went in the pool house to see what was in the refrigerator. He came back out and said, 'Score! Look what I found! Banana pudding, my favorite!' He brought out two cups, one for him and one for Jubilee. He ate all of his, but Jubilee didn't finish hers. She said it tasted funny."

"Did you have any?"

"I had an ice pop. I don't like banana pudding."

"How long after they ate it before they got sick?"

"I don't know. Maybe an hour? Uncle Trainor kept saying he was thirsty. He got out of the water to get something to drink, but before he could, he had a seizure."

"Aha! I think we're onto something here," Hoopsinger told Agent Burns. "Looks like the banana pudding's our culprit."

"Possibly, but don't rush to conclusions. Wait and see what they say at the hospital," Burns suggested.

Hoopsinger was a firm believer in the principle of theory construction known as Occam's razor. She was convinced that it had to be the pudding. The two people who ate it became sick, while a third person who abstained from having any remained healthy. Ergo, it must be the pudding. It was neat. It was simple. It made sense. She asked Benjamin, "Where did it come from?"

"Louetta made it, Louetta Waites. She's the cook here. There was some for dessert at lunch. Uncle Trainor had some, and Jubilee, and Aunt Palmer, and I think my mom and Aunt Yamma did, but nobody got sick. Benjamin paused, thinking it over, then his eyes widened. "If it made Uncle Trainor and Jubilee sick because there was something bad in it, whatever it was must have been put in after lunch."

Hoopsinger gave Agent Burns an amused sidelong look, as if to say, "Get a load of this! A kid's playing detective." Self-importantly adjusting her duty belt, she told Benjamin, "Leave it to the professionals to draw conclusions. We're trained for it. You're not. Now, I need to talk to Ms. Waites so I can create a timeline about the whereabouts of that pudding between when y'all ate lunch and when y'all went swimming."

Louetta was in the kitchen, preparing to cater a wedding reception. She had called in reinforcements in the form of three women from Cobbs. They were putting together platters of grilled steak salad, oysters, shrimp, devilled eggs, and a mouth-watering assortment of canapés.

Louetta could provide no information about the banana pudding, other than to state unequivocally that there was nothing wrong with it.

As proof, she removed a mixing bowl containing the pudding from the walk-in cooler and placed it with an angry thump on one of the marble countertops. Before Hoopsinger could stop her, she spooned some into a cereal bowl and ate a spoonful.

"See? I ain't poisoned," she said. "Watch, Ima have some more. Nope, still ain't poisoned. If you think I'm some kinda Lucrezia Borgia, goin' around poisoning folks, you barkin' up the wrong tree."

She put her hands on her hips and glared, as if daring them to make something of it.

Agent Burns tried to reassure her. "No one's accusing you of anything."

"That's good, because I ain't done nothing, except work my fingers to the bone, night and day, making the best food in Boyce County."

"Amen! You got that right," said one of ladies from Cobbs.

Louetta noticed Janelle was videoing the encounter on her phone. Scowling thunderously, she threatened, "If you put that up on the internet, I'll tell your mom you been keepin' company with that no-good Stiller DuBois, ridin' around in his truck 'til all hours, drinkin' and foolin' around."

Janelle put the phone in her pocket.

"Smart girl," Louetta said.

At the hospital, Trainor and Jubilee were recovering from their ordeal. It had been a close call. Palmer told Marsh that Trainor had been lucky. Despite his having eaten an entire cup of tainted pudding, the doctors said he didn't appear to have suffered permanent brain damage.

"How could they tell?" Marsh asked. "It's Trainor, after all. He told me one time, in complete seriousness, that the moon must be closer to White Oaks than Florida is, because he could see the moon from White Oaks and he couldn't see Florida."

Palmer had chivvied the governor and the state's attorney general into making the case top-priority. The cups and spoons Hoopsinger recovered from beside the pool were put on a fast track for testing at the Georgia Bureau of Investigation's Division of Forensic Sciences laboratory in Moultrie. The results came back positive for traces of datura, a plant belonging to the highly poisonous nightshade family.

"Hells bells!" said a startled Aimee, upon hearing the news.

"That's what it's sometimes called," Marsh told her. "Angel's trumpet, devil's trumpet, hells bells; it all amounts to the same thing: a plant with pretty blossoms, but any part of which can be deadly if ingested."

"Why would anyone want to do that?"

"For the hallucinogenic effect."

Aimee shook her head. "Trainor's pulled some stupid stunts, but he'd never eat a poison plant just so he could see things that aren't there, and he'd never give any to Jubilee. Whoever put angel's trumpet in the banana pudding, it wasn't Trainor."

"I agree," Marsh said.

"And it wasn't Jubilee. She knows better. Benjamin showed her where the blackberry and raspberry bushes are, and the strawberry plants. He told her not to eat anything else in the garden unless an adult says it's okay."

"Good advice," Marsh said.

"Then who? It didn't get in the pudding by itself."

It was two days after the poolside crisis. They were in a room at White Oaks which was done up like an old-fashioned ice cream parlor. Blanton had it created as a gift for his first wife, a Hollywood starlet. She'd appeared in a film in a minor role as a waitress who served sodas and ice cream to frolicsome high school students. Blanton had the set recreated at White Oaks, down to the jukebox filled with records, the college pennants on the walls, and the long, marble-topped counter with shining brass fittings.

Yamma was behind the counter making an ice cream treat. She scooped vanilla ice cream into a blender, added eggs, grape syrup, and shaved ice, blending it until it until it was smooth. She poured the purple mixture into tall, fluted glasses, added a spritz of seltzer water, then topped her creation with whipped cream and a drizzle of grape syrup.

"Here, try this," she said, as she brought two glasses to the vinyl-upholstered booth where Aimee and Marsh were seated. "It's a Catawba Flip. Your Uncle Courtland and I were introduced to it at a cute little place on the Outer Banks. I'm going to make one for Jubilee when she gets out of the hospital. She loves anything purple."

Agent Burns entered the room, having been directed to it by Louetta. She looked around, surprised. "You really do have an ice cream parlor here. I thought Louetta was joking."

Marsh patted the seat next to him. "Please, sit. We have all kinds of things at White Oaks. I'll show you the bowling alley later."

"Naturally there's a bowling alley. No home would be complete without one. Do you have a bookcase that swings out to reveal a hidden passageway?"

"As a matter of fact, we do. Care for a Catawba Flip?"

"Is that what those are called? Thanks, I could use something sweet right about now," Burns said. She was exhausted. It had been a rough couple of days.

"Was the crime lab able to find any fingerprints on the cups and spoons?" Aimee asked.

"Only Trainor's and Jubilee's. Palmer said Jubilee had her fingerprints taken as part of a school safety program. Trainor was fingerprinted when he applied to volunteer at Jubilee's school. Whoever tampered with the banana pudding must have worn gloves," Burns said.

Trainor's school volunteering ended abruptly as the result of a slide presentation he gave to Jubilee's class. The youngsters had enjoyed the classic children's book *Make Way for Ducklings,* which recounts the adventures of a mother duck seeking a safe place to raise her eight ducklings. The children were eager to learn more about ducks, and Trainor was glad to oblige.

The slide show began peacefully enough, with a flock of ducks flying above a pond fringed with cattails.

"See there? Those're the same kind of ducks as the ones in the storybook. Ain't they pretty? They're called mallards," Trainor told the rapt children.

He uncapped an erasable marker. On a whiteboard he wrote DUCK, POND, and SWIM in large, straggling letters.

"Those words are gonna be on your spelling test. Your teacher told 'em to me, and I'm learning 'em to you, so you can do good on the test," Trainor told the children.

"How many ducks are there?" he asked, when they finished copying the words in their notebooks. "Let's count 'em together, out loud."

The teacher smiled as the children counted the ducks. Mr. Trapnell was doing a good job of keeping the class engaged. He even managed to integrate spelling and arithmetic into his lesson. He was a natural at this.

"That's right, there's eight of 'em," Trainor said, when the children finished counting. "Hey! You know what? Maybe they're the same baby ducks from the storybook, all growed up!"

The next slide showed the ducks landing in the pond. The children oohed and aahed. "They found a new home. They're going to live in that pond forever and ever," exclaimed a delighted little girl.

That was not to be the case, as evidenced by what transpired in the following slide. A group of men popped up from a blind and were blasting away at the ducks with shotguns. Several of the children went into hysterics.

"They're killing the ducks from *Make Way for Ducklings,*" a little boy screeched, his face twisted in a rictus of horror.

"No, they ain't," Trainor told him sternly. "Get ahold of yourself. Them ducks is the storybook was made up. They was never alive in the first place."

"Never alive? Never alive? The poor baby ducks were never alive," wept another little boy.

"Jeez, simmer down. Storybooks are made up, okay? If you believe everything you read in storybooks you're gonna be in for a rude awakening. And just so you know, the Easter Bunny and the Tooth Fairy ain't real either. Neither is Santy Claus," Trainor said, setting off another round of wails.

"What are y'all so mad about?" a bewildered Trainor asked the teacher and the assistant principal, who had been summoned to help calm the weeping, screaming children. "You mad about them ducks gettin' shot? That's what you're supposed to do to ducks. They're good eatin'. Ain't you never ate duck?"

Thus ended Trainor's brief career as a school volunteer.

Yamma asked, "Is there any angel's trumpet growing in the gardens here?"

Agent Burns said there was; she had checked with the head gardener.

"The gardeners know about it? And they know it's poisonous?" Yamma licked whipped cream from her spoon. "My goodness, you'd think they'd get rid of it."

Marsh looked thoughtful. "It's an ornamental shrub. It's only dangerous if ingested. There are several kinds of plants growing here that are toxic to humans and animals. I suppose we could post warning signs out on the grounds, the way we do in the conservatories."

Yamma pursed her lips. She hesitated, as if unsure whether to speak, before addressing Agent Burns. "You said whoever handled the cups and spoons besides Trainor and Jubilee must have worn gloves?"

Burns nodded. "That's right."

"I noticed the gardeners all wear gloves. Do you suppose one of them might have a grudge against the Trapnells and... Oh, I don't like saying it." Yamma covered her mouth with her hand, her eyes wide, as if shocked by her own words.

Burns had interviewed the gardeners and groundskeepers. They all seemed satisfied with their jobs. None of them struck her as a potential poisoner. According to Lee, none of the staff, indoors or out, had been fired since he began working there.

Aimee saw where Yamma was going with this. "Might have what? Poisoned the pudding because they hate my family? That's ridiculous. How would they know one of us would eat it? Anyone could have gone in the pool house and helped themselves. We encourage the outdoor staff to take bottled water and anything else they want from the refrigerator. It prevents them from bothering Louetta. It doesn't make sense that one of them would have done it."

"I suppose you're right, dear," Yamma said. "I was just thinking aloud. It was foolish of me."

CHAPTER SIXTEEN
NIGHTY-TIGHTY

Sales of Night Garden perfume continued to skyrocket. The launch of Aimee's skincare line was soon to take place, at a secret location to be revealed at the last moment on Aimee's Instagram. One hundred of her lucky followers who correctly guessed the location would receive gift bags containing quarter-ounce bottles of Night Garden; a sleep mask emblazoned with the slogan "Night Garden: It Will Transform You;" a ghost-written book entitled *Aimee Trapnell's Guide to Beautiful Living,* and a skincare product called Cultivar Glo.

The advertising copy for Cultivar Glo breathlessly announced, "Introducing a breakthrough scientific advance in skincare unlike any other. Suffused with precious macronutrients, Aimee Trapnell's Cultivar Glo gives skin a dewy-fresh, rose-petal glow that lifts and tightens without needles or surgery."

Whether the macronutrients in Cultivar Glo were precious was open to debate. They were common elements, including calcium, potassium, and magnesium, all of which are essential for plant health, but have little effect when rubbed on human skin. They appeared in trace amounts in Cultivar Glo, the main ingredient of which was water, followed by glycerin.

While a three-ounce jar would retail for one hundred and fifteen dollars, the ingredients therein cost pennies. The jar itself was the big lure. It resembled the vaguely intimidating glassware found in research laboratories, the unspoken message being that Cultivar Glo was cutting-edge science, rather than a run-of-the-mill moisturizer, no different from any sold in discount drugstores.

Aimee was on the balcony outside her room at White Oaks. She was testing a new item for her skincare line, an undereye treatment called Nighty-Tighty.

The instructions on the box said Nighty-Tighty should be dabbed on the undereye area before retiring for the night. By morning it would have done its miraculous work, making the skin under the user's eyes, "fresh and bright, noticeably reducing the appearance of wrinkles and dark circles."

Aimee was too impatient to smear the goo under her eyes before going to bed and leaving it on overnight. She was primarily concerned with how it smelled and how it felt when she patted it on her skin. It had a clean, eucalyptus scent, which was good, but she wasn't sure about its consistency.

She fetched the jar from her dressing table, where it had been since she unpacked the box of sample products sent for her to try. She brought it outside to the balcony. Looking out over the gardens, she repeated her action of the past few days by leaning against the iron railing and applying Nighty-Tighty beneath her eyes.

The railing gave way with a metallic groan. It fell with a crash to the ground far below. Aimee barely managed not to fall along with it, jerking herself away from the edge just in time. She stumbled, knocking over the table where she'd placed her water bottle and cell phone. She realized to her horror that she couldn't see. Her eyes were sealed shut.

She groped on the floor, fearful of going in the wrong direction and falling through the gap created by the broken railing. Crawling on her hands and knees, she felt for the handle of the French door leading to her room. She bumped her head, hard, shattering one of the glass panes. Blood ran down her face from a deep gash on her forehead.

"Ow, shit," she swore, and raised her voice, "Help! Somebody help me! I'm blind! I'm bleeding! Goddammit, this sucks!"

"Everyone's going to the hospital, first Uncle Trainor and Jubilee and now Mom," Benjamin remarked to Agent Burns several hours later. Marsh had driven Aimee to the emergency room, where the laceration on her forehead was stitched and her eyelids were gently pried open. Trainor and Jubilee were still in the hospital, having been moved from intensive care to separate step-down units. That made three members of the Trapnell family hospitalized in the same week.

"It's probably just a coincidence," Burns told Benjamin, although privately, she wondered.

At the hospital, an intern scolded Aimee, "You shouldn't glue your eyes shut."

"I didn't," Aimee said.

The intern consulted her notes. "It says here you reported on intake that you rubbed glue on your eyes."

"That's a lie," Aimee protested. "I told them I used a skincare product that glued my eyes shut. I used it before and it never did that. Someone must have tampered with it."

Aimee was seated on a padded examining table inside a curtained cubicle just off the emergency room's waiting area. The protective sheet of paper beneath her crackled as she shifted impatiently. Experiencing a medical emergency tends to make people humble and pathetically grateful for any assistance given to them, but not Aimee. She glared at the intern through fiery red eyes. The line of sutures on her forehead did nothing to improve her malignant appearance.

"Do you suspect someone, or perhaps a group of individuals, of plotting against you?" the intern asked.

"I'm not crazy, if that's what you're getting at. That's the kind of question you ask crazy people."

"We don't like to use that word. We prefer saying someone is emotionally or mentally ill and in need of treatment."

With dignity, Aimee said she was neither of those things and could she go home now?

She could, the intern said, but it would be best to stay until she could be examined by the ophthalmologist on staff, to make sure she hadn't scratched her corneas or otherwise injured her eyes.

"When will that be?" Aimee asked.

"Tomorrow. The ophthalmologist is attending a medical conference. He'll be back in tomorrow," the intern said, lying through her teeth. The ophthalmologist was with a group of other physicians, but they weren't at a medical conference. They were at a bachelor party in one of the casino hotels in Shreveport, Louisiana, and were in no condition to function on any but the most primitive level.

"We'll get you admitted and then you can have a nice rest," the intern said.

"All right, but I want a private room. I don't share rooms with strangers. I want the best room you've got. I don't eat hospital food, so don't bother bringing me any. My brother will bring me meals prepared by our cook. I will have a cup of coffee, however. Get someone to bring me one, right now. Make sure it's regular coffee, not decaffeinated. I hate decaffeinated coffee," Aimee said, adding threateningly, "The stitches you put in my forehead better not leave a scar."

The intern went to the nurses' station to have Aimee admitted. She remarked, sotto voce, to a nurse, "The patient in exam room four is a real prima donna."

"That's one of the Trapnells. They're like royalty around here," the nurse informed her.

Marsh visited with Trainor while Aimee was being treated. Trainor was in good spirits. He was sitting up in bed, eating crackers and watching a game show on TV.

"They said I ate enough poison to kill ten men," Trainor said proudly. "I been thinkin' about doin' something nice for this hospital, as a reward for savin' my life. I phoned Dooley and he said I could buy some new X-ray machines, or maybe I could build a whole new wing. He said it's called philanthropy, and get this! It's tax deductible! I got Holt Whittaker at the bank lookin' into it. He says I can get 'em to name it after me. They can put, 'This here wing was generously donated by Trainor Scott Trapnell' in big letters on the front, so everybody knows what a good thing I done."

Jubilee was in the pediatric unit, her foul mood contrasting with the cheery décor, which featured a ballet and football motif, intended to appeal to both girls and boys. Jubilee was furious because Palmer had confessed to having returned Sheldon, the snapping turtle, to the swamp.

"He wasn't happy living in a terrarium. He belongs in the swamp, with his turtle friends. You wouldn't like living in a terrarium all by yourself, would you?" Palmer asked.

"I would so! I would so like living in a terrarium all by myself. Damn you to Hell, Mommy," Jubilee shrieked, causing the little girl who shared the room with her, and the little girl's parents, who were visiting, to gasp.

"I don't think you would," said Palmer.

"I would! You're mean! Wait until I tell Daddy you put Sheldon in the swamp. Sheldon loves me. He'll miss me! He's scared of the animals in the swamp!"

Palmer doubted that. "Sheldon's built like a tank. He bites. The animals in the swamp are scared of Sheldon."

Jubilee screamed in outrage. She seized the bed rail and shook it, kicking her legs.

"Don't do that; you're rumpling the sheets. The nurses have enough to do, without having to come in here and fix your sheets," Palmer told her.

Jubilee bared her teeth and snarled, looking as if she were demonically possessed. "I don't care," she hissed. "I'll rumple them if I feel like it. I'll rumple them and rumple them and rumple them. I'll never quit rumpling them. So there!"

Palmer left, thinking how, at times like this, Jubilee bore an uncanny resemblance to Blanton, her irascible grandfather. She kept that thought to herself, telling Jubilee only that she would return when she calmed down and stopped acting like a baby.

CHAPTER SEVENTEEN
ALOZ AND BENJAMIN DISAPPEAR

Special Agent Carson Burns was beginning to suspect something was amiss at White Oaks. First, Yamma almost fell off the tower in the garden, then Trainor and Jubilee were poisoned, then Aimee's eyes were glued shut. Burns had examined the balcony railing and found the screws holding a section in place had been removed. By leaning against it, Aimee had caused it to come loose, with what could have been disastrous results.

Yamma had apologized to Aloz for bumping into him on the tower. She shame-facedly explained that her balance wasn't as good as it once was, and she'd felt dizzy.

"Is okay," the ersatz valet assured her. "Age happens to all who are fortunate to live a long time, and who do not die young from disease, or from being slain by their enemies."

"Or as the result of an unfortunate accident, such as what happened to Trainor and little Jubilee, or from product tampering," Yamma said, referring to the Aimee's mishap with the Nighty-Tighty. "I hate to think about what they went through. They're in my prayers, the poor things."

Agent Burns thought Marsh was right in his suggestion that the cement holding the stone in place atop the tower must have crumbled due to age and weather, but the pudding had obviously been sabotaged. So had the railing. So had Aimee's eye cream. A sample sent to the GBI laboratory in Moultrie showed it contained ethyl-2 cyanoacrylate, an adhesive used in making instant glue. Aimee could have been blinded.

Burns concluded that the threat to the Trapnells was real, but who was behind it?

Aimee was still hospitalized, having developed a painful rash from the tainted eye cream. She was being cared for by her Manhattan dermatologist, who had been flown in at Aimee's expense and awarded temporary privileges at the hospital in Pontahatcha. The hospital administrators understood that it was in their best interest to acquiesce to whatever demands Aimee made.

Besides, Trainor Trapnell intended to give the hospital a new wing. He and Jubilee were about to be released in a few days. Feverish preparations were underway for a farewell party for them, with dancing to a live orchestra and speeches by the hospital's board of trustees. Attendance would be mandatory for all staff.

Agent Burns and Marsh were discussing the events of the past few days in the gardens behind White Oaks. There was a warm, gentle breeze. The evening air was deliciously scented with fresh-mown grass, jasmine, and bougainvillea.

An indigo bunting, its feathers a metallic, lapis blue, flew out of the yew hedges making up the maze and landed on a bird feeder. Finding it occupied by a male cardinal who seemed about to assert his territorial rights, the smaller bird moved on to try its luck at another of the bird feeders scattered throughout the grounds.

Agent Burns and Marsh stood talking beside the water cascade. Sheets of water pumped from the swamp flowed endlessly over its granite steps. Looking around at the serene beauty of the gardens, Burns thought White Oaks would be paradise, were it not for the anxiety-provoking presence of the Trapnells.

Burns didn't like recalling her last phone conversation with Special Supervisory Agent Ronald DiFranco. He had been displeased to learn that three of the Trapnells were in the hospital.

"You were supposed to protect them. Why did you let them get poisoned and blinded?" he demanded.

"This is a big place, sir. There's no security. None. Anybody can get in," she said. She hesitated to give him the really bad news, but there was no way around it.

"The teenager? Aimee Trapnell's son? He's gone, sir."

DiFranco blew his top. "Gone? What the fuck do you mean he's gone? Where did he go?"

"Italy, sir."

Over the phone's little speaker Burns could hear furious thumping. She felt an ice-cold wire of fear twist in her belly when she realized it was the sound of DiFranco beating his fists on his desk. An angry DiFranco was bad juju. It could mean she would be sent back to the Bozeman field office in disgrace, her career with the bureau effectively dead.

DiFranco shouted, "Italy? Are you fucking kidding me? You let him go to Italy? Why? What got into you? I told you to keep them all at that goddamn mansion, didn't I? Why is he in Italy? What possible reason would he have to go to Italy? Jesus Christ, Agent Burns! What were you thinking?"

Burns had come to realize that keeping an eye on the Trapnells was like trying to herd cats. She was powerless over them. The Trapnells did whatever they felt like doing.

"His father lives in Italy, sir. He's a count who designs knitwear. He and the boy's mother are divorced. He invited the boy to come for a visit."

"A knitwear-designing count? Must be some kind of weirdo. And you let the kid go?"

Burns braced herself. "I didn't let him go. He and the valet were gone before I knew anything about it."

"What valet?"

"Marsh Trapnell's valet, sir. Guy by the name of Aloz Olak."

"What kind of name is that? Sounds like a Muslim. Why is he taking a kid that's not his out of the country? Oh, God," DiFranco moaned, struck by a terrible idea. "It's human trafficking, that's what it is. Muslim terrorism and human trafficking! My God, this is horrible! This is your fault, Agent Burns."

"The boy is eighteen. He's lived on the streets. He's smart. No way is anyone taking advantage of him. I assure you, sir, it's not human trafficking. He's simply visiting his father. The valet went with him because the father is a count. He expects the boy to travel with a servant."

That was how Marsh explained it to her, when she learned that Benjamin had left. She hoped it was the truth.

It wasn't, not exactly.

Benjamin was indeed on his way to Italy in Marsh's private jet, but he and Andy had a stop to make first.

CHAPTER EIGHTEEN
THE BIG BAD WOLF

Benjamin was enjoying a grilled-cheese sandwich and a bowl of tomato-basil soup, prepared by the chef on his Uncle Marsh's private jet, when about six hours into their flight, the plane began to descend.

Jagged mountains came into view, and a long, narrow inlet. Benjamin thought it was a fjord. Italy had mountains, and there was a fjord on the Amalfi coast. Benjamin had seen it the last time he was there, after he escaped from a Swiss rehab, with the help of his Uncle Trainor. Something about this terrain struck him as unusual, however. For one thing, it appeared too sparsely populated to be Italy.

He asked one of the cabin attendants, "Are we in Italy already? That was quick."

Andy, seated in a plush, white leather seat across from him, looked out the window at the landscape rapidly coming into view below them. "Unless I am very much mistaken, that is not Italy," he said.

A puzzled Benjamin asked the cabin attendant, "Not Italy? Are we stopping somewhere? How come? I thought this plane held enough fuel to take us direct from Georgia to Italy."

"It does," she told him. "But first, Mister Trapnell has business he wants the gentleman with you to attend to in Iceland. We will be landing at Akureyri, the gateway to Iceland's Arctic North."

"Cool. I always wanted to go to Iceland. They have these steaming hot pools you can soak in that were created by volcanic activity. Dr. Ryczak, Uncle Marsh's girlfriend, told me about them.

You can see the Northern Lights from Iceland. The Northern Lights are trippy!" Benjamin said, delighted by the unexpected change in itinerary.

The airport in Akureyri was small, with a single runway. Faces could be seen pressed against the terminal windows, gaping at the giant jet with an erupting volcano on its tail as it taxied to a stop.

"Are you movie stars or something?" a customs officer, awed by the magnificent aircraft, asked Benjamin and Andy.

"It's Justin Bieber. The man with him must be his manager," a woman said. She had hurried over from where she had been tending the deserted Hertz car rental counter. She smiled hopefully at Benjamin. "May I take a selfie with you, Justin? I'm a huge fan."

The customs officer examined their passports. He told the car-rental woman, "Calm down, Helga. It's not Justin Bieber. Justin Bieber is Canadian. This is an American named Benjamin Monteleone and an Ulakistani named..." He frowned, puzzling out the name written in the passport, "Andrej Yakov Temirkhan Asgarov Sadyharbaghi."

"Wait a minute! I thought you were Aloz Olek," Benjamin said to Andy.

"I have many names. I am a man of a thousand faces. They don't call me the Wizard of Wyvovik Pass for nothing," Andy told him. He puffed out his chest and glanced at the customs official and the car-rental woman to see if they were impressed.

"Well, wizard, enjoy your stay in Iceland. You too, Justin Bieber," the customs officer said with a smile, and stamped their passports.

As they walked toward the exit, Benjamin picked up a tourism brochure from one of the counters. "There's a place where you can stay in a yurt. Can we do that?" he asked Andy.

Andy made a disgusted face. "Yurts are for hippies. I despise hippies. They are idle and self-indulgent and smell of patchouli. In my country, anyone who does yoga and wears tie-dyed clothing is sent to a forced-labor camp."

"Where are we going to stay, then?" Benjamin asked. He and Andy exited the terminal and were immediately surrounded by four men wearing camouflage. They had on mirrored sunglasses and had rifles slung over their shoulders.

"With Princess Farah of Ishran. These gentlemen work for her, at least I hope they do. If not, it would appear we are being abducted," Andy said.

"We work for the princess," the man who seemed to be the group's leader confirmed. "Come this way. Princess Farah is at the compound, waiting to greet you."

Another of the men chimed in, "We love the princess. We would give our lives for her."

"But we probably won't have to," the first man reassured Benjamin and Andy. "Anybody who messes with us will get blown into little pieces the size of golf balls. Let's go!"

Benjamin and Andy got into the first in a line of four identical black Range Rovers. Then the vehicles sped away.

"These men are mercenaries, and good ones, I think. Don't worry," Andy whispered to Benjamin.

"I'm not worried. This is baller! We're part of an armed convoy, on our way to see a princess. Iceland is even better than I thought," Benjamin said.

The driver grinned at him. "You want to see something good? Watch that traffic light up ahead."

The convoy approached a traffic signal. The light had turned red. Benjamin was interested to see it was in the shape of a glowing red heart. The driver pressed something on the dashboard and the light instantly changed to green, allowing them to drive through the intersection without stopping.

"Mobile infrared transmitter," the driver said. "It's an electronic device that preempts traffic control signals. Emergency vehicles like ambulances and fire trucks have them, as well as all the princess' vehicles. It's not exactly condoned for use by private citizens, but the princess has done good things for the economy and so we're allowed to have it. That way, we can go through intersections without stopping, in case some asshole is lying in wait, intending to ambush us."

"Cool," said Benjamin. "Does that happen often? The ambushing?"

"Often enough. The religious fanatics who murdered Princess Farah's family won't quit until they kill her, too. It's some kind of ideological thing."

"Wow, I feel bad for her," Benjamin said. "So, how come that red light back there was shaped like a heart?"

"You noticed that, huh? It's part of a morale-boosting campaign called Smile With Your Heart. The city started it during the 2008 financial crisis. People were encouraged to make hearts and display them, to cheer everybody up and make them forget that the economy was in the toilet."

"Did it work?' Benjamin asked.

"Yep," the driver replied. "The hearts became a symbol of Akureyri. The tourists like them, and the economy improved, so it's all good."

Akureyri reminded Benjamin of small cities he had been to in Scandinavia. The same jagged mountains, the same peaked-roofed buildings painted in bright, primary colors, the same fishing fleet bobbing at anchor in the harbor, no graffiti, no litter, everything neat and tidy.

"Nice place," said Andy.

"It is," the driver agreed. "It gets a little nippy, with the Arctic Circle only about sixty miles away, but it has a lot going for it. There's a vibrant nightlife, and with it being so far north, any Ishrani assassins stick out like sore thumbs, coming from a desert region the way they do. They're not used to the cold. It freaks them out. I'm from southern California myself and I had a hard time getting used to the climate. Still, it's a good gig. The princess pays well and I get to go hiking and rock climbing on my days off."

"You're from California? I wondered how come you speak such good English," Benjamin said.

"The schools here teach English as a second language. A lot of people speak it," the driver said. He pulled off the Ring Road, the highway which encircles the country, and onto a dirt track barely wider than the Range Rovers. After several bumpy miles it ended at a high cement wall topped with razor wire. The convoy pulled up to a formidable metal gate posted with No Trespassing signs in several languages. Their driver spoke into a radio.

"Big Bad Wolf, this is Cheeseburger. We are 10-99, over."

The radio crackled as a muffled voice said, "Big Bad Wolf to Cheeseburger. Is everything five by five? Over."

"Affirmative. We're five-by, over."

"Come on in, boys. Over and out," the voice crackled.

The gate swung open and the convoy rolled through.

Princess Farah had been granted asylum in Iceland following the overthrow of her father's government. The compound where she resided was less a palace and more of a fortress. There were machine gun emplacements on the roof. A brace of closed-circuit security cameras above the steel door in front watched Benjamin and Andy as they disembarked from the Range Rover.

The door rolled up to reveal a cement-floored, steel-walled courtyard. Three women stood facing them. Two were large and tough-looking. The third was shorter and slighter than her companions, but she appeared equally capable of handling herself. Her sharp features relaxed in a welcoming smile upon sight of her guests.

"I'm Princess Farah. Welcome! I'm so glad you stopped by. We don't get many visitors. Permit me to introduce Maryam and Samira, my ladies-in-waiting."

"Hi," said Maryam.

"How ya doing?" said Samira.

"You're the Big Bad Wolf," Benjamin said, having recognized the princess' voice.

"I am indeed," she laughed. "Your Uncle Marsh suggested that handle. He has a marvelous sense of humor. How is he, by the way?"

"He's fine. He said to say hello." Then Benjamin remembered his manners. Gesturing to Andy, he said, "This is, uh, I'm not sure what his real name is. He used to be Uncle Marsh's valet."

Andy bowed. "I am not a valet. That was merely a clever ruse. I am Andrej Yakov Temirkhan Asgarov Sadyharbaghi, former beloved president of the magnificent nation of Ulakistan, now temporarily forced to seek asylum elsewhere."

The princess shook his outstretched hand. "You were exiled, huh? I know the feeling."

"Only temporarily," said Andy.

"Of course. Marsh explained everything. You are welcome to stay here for as long as you like. I cleared it with the prime minister."

Andy squeezed her hand and drew her closer. "You are kind. Is it all right with your husband if I stay here?"

Princess Farah looked coyly at him. "Didn't Marsh tell you? I'm single."

A look of astonishment appeared on Andy's face. He raised her hand to his lips. "But how is this possible? How is it that such a beautiful and cultured lady is single? This must be fate, for I too, am currently in the market, as they say."

A meaningful silence followed as they exchanged long looks.

"You know," Andy said thoughtfully, "when I regain my rightful place as president for life of the glorious nation of Ulakistan, I shall require a wife, a beautiful helpmeet to graciously preside at my side. Naturally, she will have heaps and heaps of diamonds and whatever else she desires. What do you say? Does that sound interesting?"

Andy appeared to have conveniently forgotten he had made Aimee the same matrimonial offer.

Princess Farah smiled and lowered her eyes. "Let's get to know each other better before I give you an answer. As it happens, my intelligence sources inform me that the time is ripe to attempt a takeover of my father's kingdom, with his rightful heir–myself–as head of state. If I had a husband, one who was stern and forceful and didn't take any nonsense when he was the victim of a coup, but who made a successful comeback and punished those responsible, well, that would be very nice. For both of us." Princess Farah raised one slender, inquiring eyebrow.

Andy chuckled. "I am liking this idea very much."

Princess Farah indicated a steel door in one of the walls. "Let's go inside where it's more comfortable. This part of the house is a safe room, in case the perimeter wall and the gate are breached. It's much nicer inside. Maryam and Samira will show you to your rooms. I'm delighted you both are here!"

CHAPTER NINETEEN
AN AMAZING REVELATION

It was late afternoon, several days after Benjamin and Andy departed. Marsh and Lee Gi-yong, the butler at White Oaks, were drinking sweet tea in the mansion's kitchen. Louetta had left for the day, after mopping the floor and wiping down the countertops with a cleaning solution of her own making, leaving her domain spotless, ready for another day of preparing the best food in Boyce County, Georgia.

Lee was interested to hear that the former Aloz Olek was to be a guest of Princess Farah. He would remain at her compound in Iceland for the indeterminate future.

"For a former dictator, he made a pretty good valet," Lee told Marsh.

"He did," Marsh agreed. "I was sorry to see him go, but it was for the best. He couldn't stay here forever. He got bored at that ranch in Texas and did a flit. The government would be hard put to find somewhere to keep him where he wouldn't escape again."

Lee looked thoughtful. "There's always Guantánamo Bay."

Marsh swirled the ice cubes in his glass. "I don't think a military prison would be an appropriate place to house a foreign dignitary, even one who was deposed because he employed rather extreme methods in governing his country."

Lee finished his tea and got up to leave. He rinsed his glass and placed it in the sink. "I'd better shove off. Unless there's anything you need?"

"No, you go on home. Palmer is at the hospital, with Trainor and Jubilee and Aimee. They were pronounced fully cured today, thanks to the miracle of modern medicine, or such as it can be said to exist at Pontahatcha General Hospital.

The hospital is throwing a shindig for them tonight, to thank Trainor for agreeing to donate a new wing. It's just me and Agent Burns here, and Yamma. We can dine on cold fried chicken and play cards or something. I'll see you tomorrow."

Marsh heard Lee's steps retreating down the cypress-floored hallway, followed by the sound of the front door closing. The huge old house fell silent, except for the quiet purr of the walk-in cooler. Marsh poured himself another glass of sweet tea. He cocked his head at the sound of footsteps coming down the back stairs.

Agent Burns appeared through the doorway leading from the kitchen corridor.

"I just got off the phone with my supervisor," she said.

"Oh, really? Care for some sweet tea?"

"No. Would you like to know what he said?"

Marsh smiled agreeably. "Do tell."

"He said the former president of Ulakistan, who used to be staying at a ranch in Texas that's owned by federal government, is now in Iceland. No one can figure out how he got there." Burns folded her arms.

"My goodness! How mysterious!"

"Isn't it, though? Don't you have a friend who lives in Iceland?

Marsh took a drink of tea before replying. "Now that you mention it, I do."

"Isn't your friend named Princess Farah of Ishran?"

"Now that you mention it, my friend in Iceland is named Princess Farah of Ishran."

Burns smiled wickedly. "This is going to blow your mind, but that's who the former president of Ulakistan is staying with, your pal Princess Farah."

"How nice for him," said Marsh. "The princess is a gracious hostess. No doubt this Ulakistani fellow will enjoy staying with her."

"Yeah, he probably will. Say, how are Benjamin and that valet of yours doing in Italy?"

"They're having a fine time. Benjamin's father has a place in Milan, as well as a villa in Sardinia, on the Costa Smeralda. That's where they are now. The weather's been fantastic. They go to the beach every day."

Burns seated herself at the kitchen table and folded her hands. "Oh, really? Benjamin and that guy you claimed was your valet are both in Italy right now?"

Marsh's brow wrinkled in perplexity. "That's what I said. My nephew, Benjamin, and my valet, Aloz Olek, are in Italy."

"Oh, give it up, Bad Choices. Don't you ever get tired of telling lies? There is no such person as Aloz Olek. Aloz Olek doesn't exist."

A look of puzzled concern crossed Marsh's handsome face. "Are you feeling quite well, Agent Burns? Of course he exists. You met him."

"I met someone you said was him. It wasn't. It was a guy called Andrej Sadyharbaghi, who just happens to be the former president of Ulakistan."

"Are you saying my valet was this Andrej person? I had no idea. I'm stunned."

Burns burst into laughter at Marsh's look of incredulity. "Stop pretending that this comes as a shock. You're busted. Not only was your fake valet the former president of Ulakistan, you arranged for him to go to Iceland, on your big-ass private jet."

Realizing the game was up, Marsh said, "Oh, dear. I suppose the FBI is angry with me, is that what you're trying to say? Am I about to be indicted? Will I need legal representation? Should I call Dooley Voight?"

Burns held up her hand, palm out. "Nope. You're not being indicted. Not this time, anyway. My boss said it's good news that Sadyharbaghi is now Iceland's problem instead of ours. He's been granted asylum there."

"It seems our troubles are over," said Marsh. "Are you sure you don't want some sweet tea?' He was reaching for the pitcher to refill his glass when a voice spoke up.

"Put your hands up, both of you. Agent Burns, remove your sidearm, if you please, slowly. Now, place it on the floor. Good. Push it gently toward me. That's right. Keep your hands where I can see them. Shit, as they say, is about to get real."

It was Yamma. She was pointing a gun at Marsh's head.

CHAPTER TWENTY
AN ANCIENT GRIEVANCE

The mild-mannered old lady had undergone a startling metamorphosis. Sneering, her normally benign blue eyes flinty, Yamma had revealed a new and unpleasant side to herself. She bent to pick up Burns' sidearm. Keeping her eyes on the FBI agent, she placed it on one of the marble-topped counters. She wore sturdy brown gloves, like those used by the gardeners on the estate. Her hand was steady, the gun aimed at a point between Marsh's eyes.

Marsh found his throat had gone dry. He swallowed and said, "Aimee said you had a gun."

"And here it is," Yamma replied.

"Ms. Castleberry, please, put the gun down and let's talk," Agent Burns began, but Yamma cut her off.

"Shut up, you," she growled. "Shut up and listen. I have something to say and I mean to say it, without interruption, d'you hear?"

Agent Burns and Marsh nodded their heads.

"White Oaks should be mine," Yamma declared. "It's not fair that nasty old Blanton got it instead of his brother, Courtland. Courtland's mother, that bitch, never liked me."

"I don't see why not; you're charming," said Marsh.

Yamma's eyes narrowed. "Would you like a bullet in the knee, smartass?"

"No, ma'am," Marsh replied.

Glowering, Yamma went on, "I was here only once before now, shortly after Courtland and I were married. His mother never invited me back, and Courtland wouldn't press the issue. It was, 'I don't want to upset Mama. She'll come around, just give her time,' but she didn't come around. Then Courtland passed away. Even then, I wasn't welcome here. His mama came to the funeral and gave me the dirtiest look. She was a grade-A bitch."

"I won't argue with you about that," Marsh said.

Yamma's frown deepened. "Keep talking and I'll shoot you in both knees."

"Sorry, please continue," Marsh said.

"No more interruptions, or else," the old lady warned. "Where was I? Oh, yes, then the bitch died, after practically living forever, the way bitches like her tend to do. And wouldn't you know it? She left White Oaks to Blanton. There was a codicil in her will, leaving furniture and jewelry and money and whatnot to various people, but there wasn't a word about me. I might as well not have existed. Oh, I know, Courtland passed away before his mother did, but she could have given him White Oaks anyway, don't you see? She could have given it to him, and then I would own it, when he died, but no, Blanton was her golden boy. Blanton got White Oaks, and now it belongs to you, Marsh, to you and your disgusting siblings."

Marsh thought of Aimee and Trainor, two of his so-called disgusting siblings, and of Palmer and little Jubilee. They would return to White Oaks after the party at the hospital What did Yamma intend to do then?

She didn't give him long to wonder. She said, "I'll kill them. It will be easy; they won't be expecting it. That will be after I've killed you, and Agent Burns, here. Then I'll throw both guns in the swamp and go up to my room. In the morning, the servants will discover the carnage brought about by a home invasion. They'll find me, a helpless, frightened old lady, cowering in my room."

She nodded at Burns. "You'll be collateral damage, I'm sorry to say. You're not a Trapnell. I have nothing personal against you, but it's what you get for being involved with that one, there."

She jerked her chin at Marsh. Her hand holding the gun, rock steady up to that point, began to tremble. Marsh braced himself to dive toward her and tackle her before she could fire.

Out of the corner of her eye, Agent Burns saw movement. A bookcase filled with cookbooks was slowly and silently swinging forward, as if on hinges. Aha! That must be the hidden door disguised as a bookcase, which Marsh had mentioned. Yamma had her back to it, and didn't notice it moving.

Burns looked to Marsh, to see if he saw it, too. He inclined his head, signifying that he did. Burns held her breath, hoping Yamma wouldn't notice the approaching bookcase. She didn't. It hit her square in the back, making her stumble. Quick as a flash, Burns was on her. Yamma shrieked as if she were being scalded as they struggled for the gun.

Burns shoved Yamma against one of the counters, knocking the wind out of her. The old lady's knees buckled, but she retained her grip on the gun. She swept her other arm back, knocking over a radio and sending a ceramic cannister of flour to the floor. Shards of pottery flew everywhere, as a cloud of flour rose and engulfed the two women locked in a life-or-death struggle.

The radio fell flat on the counter, depressing the power button. Baby Patty Cake's voice blared out, screaming a verse from her hit song, "THOT":

"Show her a dolla if you wanna make her holla! She do anything you say, just so long as you pay!"

Marsh fumbled for the dagger in the sheath on his belt, then changed his mind and went for the heavy-duty, stainless-steel meat tenderizer mallet in the drawer where Louetta kept an assortment of potentially deadly kitchen implements.

Anea and Janelle emerged from the hidden passageway behind the bookcase. They gaped at the tussle taking place. Anea said, "Hey! The FBI lady is fighting Miz Castleberry."

"How come?" Janelle asked her.

"I don't know, but they're really going at it. Look at this mess, flour all over the floor and one of the cannisters is busted. Louetta's gonna be ill as a hornet. And look! Miz Castleberry's got a gun! This is crazy." Anea took out her phone and videoed the action.

Marsh approached the struggling women, mallet upraised, ready to strike as soon as he had a clear shot at Yamma, but before he could deliver a blow, Agent Burns managed to subdue her. She pinned her to the floor and grabbed the gun.

"Take it," she ordered Marsh.

He did, tucking it into his belt.

Burns blinked to clear her vision from the film of flour clinging to her eyelashes. She could feel her heart thumping wildly. *I can't believe what just happened,* she thought.

"How come y'all was fighting?' Janelle asked.

"Was Miz Castleberry fixin' to shoot y'all? How come?" Anea asked.

"She has an ancient grievance against my family," said Marsh.

"Like in *Game of Thrones?*" Anea asked.

"Something like that," said Marsh, replacing the mallet in the drawer and turning off the radio. "I thought you went home."

"We was roller skating in the basement. Y'all got a skating rink down there, with a sound system rigged up with top-one-hundred hits from the sixties and seventies, and a disco ball, and strobe lights and everything," Janelle said.

"I'd forgotten about that. Daddy had it installed for my stepsister, Karen. She was wild about roller skating at one point. That was before she moved to Nepal. I'll have to remind her about it, the next time we speak," said Marsh.

"Could you save the reminiscing for another time? I need you to call the sheriff and have him send somebody to take charge of Ms. Castleberry," Agent Burns said. She was breathing hard, struggling to keep Yamma pinned down as the old lady whipped her head back and forth, attempting to bite Burns' wrist.

"Stop resisting," Burns told her.

Yamma snarled, "You'll be sorry. I'm going to sue you for every cent you've got."

"Go ahead," Burns told her wearily. To Anea, she said, "Delete that video."

CHAPTER TWENTY-ONE
HOME AGAIN

The daily flower deliveries to Aimee's apartment at the Dakota resumed, her remorseful beaus having come crawling back, apologizing for their absence in the most abject of terms.

Leighton Knauss, heir to the Friendly Farmer frozen foods fortune, sent a pot of four-leaf clover, with an emerald bracelet nestled in it. An attached note said: "Forgive me please! I'm begging on my knees!"

Her other suitor, Avery Panko, tucked an invitation written in elegant calligraphy on thick, creamy stationery, asking her to join him for a weekend in Paris, at the Ritz, in with his customary offering of long-stemmed red roses.

Aimee couldn't be happier.

She would let them sweat for a while, as she enjoyed their frenzied attempts to make it up to her for having deserted her in the wake of the murders of the two hitmen in Georgia.

Yamma confessed to killing them in self-defense, saying she feared for her life when they trespassed in the field where she was tending her second husband's grave. How an old lady could overpower two professional gunmen was puzzling, although it was conjectured that she took them by surprise, with them never suspecting she was armed until it was too late.

Equally puzzling was why the gunmen were there in the first place. There was no more mention in the news of Yamma's first husband, Courtland Trapnell, or of any of the Trapnells. That was fine with Aimee.

There was also no mention of Yamma holding Marsh and an FBI agent at gunpoint. There was similarly no mention of her attempting to poison Trainor and Jubilee, or of her tampering with Aimee's eye cream, or of trying to push a valet off a tower, having mistaken him for Marsh's bodyguard. It might eventually come out, but by then enough time would have elapsed for the public to have lost interest. If Yamma had been younger and more attractive, her crimes would have been riveting, perfect fodder for a made-for-TV movie, but as she was old and wrinkled, they would merit little mention.

Yamma was currently in jail, with bail having been denied on the grounds that she was a flight risk. Her case might be postponed for a year or more. A year might as well be an eternity, as far as the news cycle was concerned. By then, more exciting crimes would have occurred and no one would care about Yamma.

Baby Patty Cake stopped mentioning the Illuminati in interviews and on her social media posts, choosing instead to go back to feuding with her nemesis, fellow rapper Platinum Champagne. That was a relief. Only crazy people believed in the Illuminati. The Illuminati didn't exist.

* * *

On a yacht anchored in the Mediterranean off Sardinia's Costa Smeralda, Count Benedetto Francesco Guillermo d'Olficcio de Monteleone was entertaining guests.

They were seated around a table in the main saloon, the crew having been ordered to remain in their quarters below deck. The huge yacht could accommodate one hundred guests, but that night they were nine in number.

The main saloon usually served as a business center, but that night, a different kind of business was taking place, one which would leave no record. The projection system was turned off, and the flat-screen TVs showed only their blank, black faces. The bartender was below, with the rest of the crew, so the count did the honors himself.

A woman, one of the Habsburgs, accepted the flute of Champagne he offered her. She asked after the count's son, doing her best to seem motherly. Although she had given birth to several children, she was not in the least maternal, as her children could unhappily attest.

"Which one? I have two sons," the count said.

"The older one. Benjamin, I believe he is called."

"He is staying with me for the summer," the count told her. "After that, he will return home to America. He is a clever boy. He seems to have gotten over his little problems and is shaping up quite satisfactorily."

"It is good to have sons," opined the Russian, tossing back a shot of vodka. "*Spasibo*," he said to the count.

"*Pozhaluysta*," the count replied. "*Drygoy?*"

The Russian nodded and the count poured him another.

The Ukrainian, who was seated next to the Russian, agreed it was indeed good to have sons, and daughters, too. Although their countries were currently at war, the Russian and the Ukrainian were the best of friends. And why not? Their friendship transcended petty annoyances such as war and national boundaries. Their friendship hinged upon their mutual involvement in what they discretely referred to as "the great matter."

"What about the Castleberry woman?" asked the Texan. He was a prominent Christian televangelist and a generous donor to conservative causes. He had managed to inculcate in his followers a terror-stricken obsession with women's restrooms and who should and should not be permitted to use them. "She's in jail. Should she be found dead one morning?"

He mimicked hanging himself, his neck at an angle, eyes crossed, tongue thrust out. The others laughed appreciatively.

"She's no threat to us. I say we leave her alone." That was an American Congresswoman, a Democrat from a state in the

Northeast. Publicly, she espoused liberal political causes and bickered viciously with the Texan, who mocked her in his broadcasts, accusing her of being "woke." Privately, they were lovers, and comrades in "the great matter."

"But she killed those hitmen we sent to take out Sadyharbaghi," the Chinese diplomat complained.

"Bad luck, that," drawled the Englishman. He was a member of the House of Lords and was friends with both sons of the current King of England. He delighted in sneakily fanning the flames of resentment between them. "He's in Iceland now. Perhaps the Ishranis will get him, along with that princess they keep trying to kill."

"I told you we should have hired better hitmen," the Chilean said with asperity. She owned a fleet of container ships. The cargo in her ships sometimes included items which were not listed on the manifest, among them uranium, which came in handy for building nuclear reactors.

"What's done is done," the Saudi told her. "Next time, *inshallah,* we may succeed." The big yacht rose with the swell of the ocean and the Saudi reached out to the inlaid teak table to rescue his beverage before it could slide off the edge.

"What's that you're drinking, my friend? the Texan asked the Saudi with a smirk.

"Apple juice. My religion forbids alcohol, as you well know; you rant about my religion often enough in your sermons to your filthy infidel followers." The Saudi punched the Texan affectionately on the arm. Then he took a sip of his apple juice, which contained a liberal amount of whiskey.

This conversation was being carried out in a variety of languages. The people gathered aboard the yacht that night were polyglots. They were of one mind and they understood each other perfectly, no matter which language was being spoken.

The Habsburg woman applied more crimson lipstick. Addressing the count, she said, "Getting back to your son, Benjamin, does he show promise, as far as joining us in the great matter is concerned?"

The count pondered. "It is too soon to tell. He is still young, but I think so, provided he is approached in the right way." He raised his glass and the others followed suit. "A toast," the count said. "To us! To the Illuminati! To our great work!"

"To the Illuminati! To our great work!" the others echoed. The room rang with the sound of their wicked, conspiratorial laughter.

THE END

ABOUT THE AUTHOR

Jill Hand is a member of International Thriller Writers. Her work has appeared in many anthologies. She is a former newspaper reporter and editor and a lifelong New Jerseyan. Her husband's family comes from Georgia. Stories he told about some of his ancestors were the inspiration for the Trapnell saga.

Red Pines is the third of her novels about the trials and tribulations of the eccentric Trapnell siblings, who have more money than is good for them.

Cobbs, home of the fictional Trapnells, is based on little towns in the Deep South, where tales of scandals from generations past are gleefully repeated over supper tables and where front porches are for sitting and fanning oneself, while complaining about the heat.

JILL HAND
WHITE
OAKS

JILL HAND
BLACK
WILLOWS

NOTE FROM JILL HAND

Word-of-mouth is crucial for any author to succeed. If you enjoyed *Red Pines*, please leave a review online—anywhere you are able. Even if it's just a sentence or two. It would make all the difference and would be very much appreciated.

Thanks!
Jill Hand

We hope you enjoyed reading this title from:

www.blackrosewriting.com

Subscribe to our mailing list – *The Rosevine* – and receive **FREE** books, daily
deals, and stay current with news about upcoming releases
and our hottest authors.
Scan the QR code below to sign up.

Already a subscriber? Please accept a sincere thank you for being a fan of
Black Rose Writing authors.

View other Black Rose Writing titles at
www.blackrosewriting.com/books and use promo code
PRINT to receive a **20% discount** when purchasing.

www.ingramcontent.com/pod-product-compliance
Lightning Source LLC
Chambersburg PA
CBHW030859200726
48289CB00003B/818